TWO DUKES IN DENMARK

STEAMY VACATION ROMANCE

INTERNATIONAL DESIRES

NC ROSS

INTRODUCTION

Trigger/CW: menage, MFM, DP, toys, sex club, discussions of a sex tape, explicit language, voyeurism

If you enjoy this book, please check out the next book in the International Desires series, *Passion in Patagonia.*

You can find all books at my website, NC Ross.

CHAPTER ONE

$\mathcal{I}$ open up the mirrored compact and inspect my eye makeup, concealer pen in hand. Not too puffy, the black of my eyeliner isn't too smudged. Perfect. You can barely tell I've been crying.

I dab here and there at the imperfections, covering them with concealer and self control.

"Everything all right?" My ride share driver asks from the front seat. He's been staring at my legs this whole time instead of the road, pervert.

"Fine, thanks." I keep my voice singsongy. After all, there's the possibility the screaming and sobbing I did earlier today would lower its natural timbre. And I'm fine. Extra fine.

The driver exits towards LaGuardia. "Which terminal?"

I tell him the name of the private jet terminal and his eyes widen. "Whoa, I'm chauffeuring a high class lady today."

I don't respond, already exhausted by this encounter. "I'm working."

He appropriately clocks my don't-fuck-with-me tone and keeps his mouth shut.

I lean back against the seat, though not so much as to

muss the French twist in my dark brown hair that I managed through my rage earlier today. *This is a good idea.* If I say it enough, it will be true, even if I have most of my vital belongings packed in my work suitcase. It's not like I'll have my own apartment to return to once this trip is over.

Tears prickle and I blink rapidly to keep them at bay. I can't mess up my waterproof mascara, but I couldn't find my setting powder in the rapid dash to leave Justin's apartment. I have to look professional. If I want this to be more than just a one-time fill-in gig for my friend Sarah, I have to pull this off. And I do. This one private flight will pay more than I earn from four of my regular commercial routes.

My phone pings and I check the lockscreen notification. Justin, again. Why can't the asshole ghost me like a normal ex? I delete the generic *can we talk?* and block his lying, cheating number.

The ride share pulls up outside the private jet terminal, and I don't make eye contact with the driver. Not after he's been ogling me in my post-break-up grief for the past half hour drive from Sarah's Brooklyn apartment.

"Have a nice flight." He whistles, and I ignore him as I roll my suitcase toward the security desk. One of the many benefits of flying private is the calm and lack of chaos that I typically see when I arrive at the airport.

"Flight crew?" The security agent asks. She has kind eyes, and for a moment, I wish I knew her better so I could confide everything to her.

"Yes." I straighten the uniform dress I borrowed from Sarah, and hand her my badge and passport. "Carolina Altshul."

She checks through my documents, then nods me along. "Denmark? Fun. Have a good flight."

I intend to. It's not like there's anything waiting for me in New York.

* * *

IT DOESN'T TAKE LONG to acquaint myself with the plane. It's a Gulfstream, built for private international travel, and this one has been decked out with the word "filthy rich" in mind. Luxurious, buttery leather, plenty of windows and leg room. Even the galley where I mix my drinks is stocked with top shelf liquor.

I'm used to observing the trappings of wealth, so I put up my mental shields as I run through the pre-flight checklist.

While I've moonlighted for this private jet company on and off over the last few years, augmenting my income from the large commercial flights I crew, I've never worked for this particular client. My bestie Sarah is one of their regular flight crew, but she was oddly tight-lipped about these people, telling me only the bare minimum.

Whatever. It's not my job to ask questions, it's my job to attend to the safety and comfort of the passengers. I am a professional, and I can manage. No one needs to know my asshole ex and I just broke up.

I stow my suitcase and pull on the apron hanging from the galley hook. Might as well get started.

The pilot, Captain Jeffers, peeks out from the cockpit. I've met her once before, but she and Sarah work together all the time. She's a beautiful, no-nonsense woman with dark brown skin and a predilection for reading non-fiction books about sailing in her free time. If I weren't reeling from heartbreak, maybe we could be friends. The co-pilot, a man with orange-tanned skin and washed-out blue eyes, hides in his seat, headphones already on. He's probably listening to music while we work.

"How are you doing, Carolina?" Captain Jeffers asks, sipping from a reusable water bottle covered in stickers from faraway places.

"Lina, please."

"I got word from the ground crew that the passenger is en route. Should be here in twenty."

I look around at the otherwise empty plane. "Is it just me on this flight?"

Captain Jeffers' brow furrows. "They didn't tell you? The other attendant called in sick. There's only one passenger, so they thought you would be fine on your own."

I straighten my shoulders. Of course, I'm always fine on my own. "No problem."

"Great." She visibly relaxes. One less thing for her to worry about. That's a big part of my job, to make shit work. Competence porn, that's me in a nutshell.

Fuck, I shouldn't be thinking about porn. Goddamn Justin and his viral sex video. Of all the—

I don't want to think about this.

I spend the next few moments waiting for the passenger to arrive. I pull my cell phone from the pocket of the half-size-too-tight dress I'm wearing. I couldn't find mine in my mad dash to get the hell out of Justin's apartment, and while Sarah and I are close in figure, my boobs and ass are just a little bigger than hers.

Nothing I can do about it now. Seven hours overnight to Copenhagen and then I can take it off, wrap myself in knits, and eat pastries for three days before I pick up a commercial flight in Stockholm. Three days is plenty of time to get my shit together. Find a new apartment. Unfollow every one of Justin's stupid dickhead social media feeds. Lie to my dads that everything is fine.

The cabin phone chimes as I'm checking the drinks. I was told the as-yet-unnamed passenger likes a cold seltzer with a sprig of rosemary and lime first thing, so I need it to be ready and on the tray when he or she arrives.

I answer the phone, cradling the receiver between my chin and shoulder. "Hello?"

"He's here."

That's all I get. I notify Captain Jeffers, and pick up the tray with the beverage in a cut crystal glass. It looks lovely, if I do say so myself. Classy and welcoming and homey.

I stand at the top of the stairs, pasting a smile on my face. I've done this thousands of times. I can greet one more bloated billionaire in a business suit.

And then I see who it is. It's *him*.

CHAPTER TWO

The tray in my hands shakes infinitesimally, but not enough to clatter the ice cubes in the seltzer.

My heart doesn't get the same "stay still" message. It's thumping so loudly in my ears, I can barely hear Captain Jeffers stepping from the cockpit and greeting him.

The man is no bloated billionaire. It's Kasper Frederiksen. I'd remember him anywhere, since he haunted my nightmares for so long.

Sure, he's twelve years older, his light brown hair shorter than it was in high school, his suit more fitted, his skin not too pale and not too tanned. He has the kind of lean body that you can tell is fit without being too muscled.

Not that I want to think about his body when the long-buried rage in my belly curdles into acid.

He won't remember me. He can't—

His gray eyes meet mine and I can see the spark of recognition. It plays low along the curves of his mouth. "Hello, Lina."

My jaw twitches, but I extend the tray toward Kasper the

Great Asshole and paste a bland smile across my red lips. "Hello, Mr. Frederiksen. Welcome on board."

Playful. The cocky asshole's expression is playful. His lips part and he runs the tip of his tongue over the planes of his perfectly white teeth. Seriously, this guy.

I jut the tray with the seltzer toward him again. "Is there anything else I can get you?" A knife in my back? I am going to kill Sarah. She must have known it would be him, and she knows exactly what this guy did to me. High school torture always extends past graduation.

Kasper's eyes flick around the interior of the plane. Damn him, those eyes are just as gold-plated and gorgeous as the rest of him. Would it kill fate to have made him uglier over the years? "Is it just us today?"

Beside me, Captain Jeffers responds, likely because I have anger lockjaw. "Yes, sir. Lina here comes highly recommended. I'm sure you'll have a safe and pleasant flight."

Kasper's lips curve into a pout. My nostrils flare. What a toddler. "Safe and pleasant. That sounds so...dull. Though I'm glad you come highly recommended."

Ugh. Why does it sound dirty when he says it? I mentally slap the tingle deep in my lower belly. I should not like this. I *know* I don't like him.

Languid, his movements slow and controlled, he lifts the crystal glass and moves into the body of the plane. He takes a seat in one of the leather chairs near the front. Great, he'll be watching me every time I use the galley to get him something. As if my day could not get worse.

Captain Jeffers turns to me. "Wheels up in ten?"

"Of course, Captain." *I'm a professional, I'm a professional, I'm a professional.*

She goes back into the cockpit and closes the door.

I check with the ground crew, but my pre-flight checklist

is complete. All that's left is to close the cabin door, which I do with an extra thud to release some of my pent-up rage.

I clench and unclench my fists. I can do this. I have to do this. It's not like I can go to a home I no longer have. I have to make this job work. Sarah gets paid nearly double what I do for flying private.

I cannot let Kasper Frederiksen, my nemesis from Viceroy Prep, get into my head.

I stride toward him and force a smile on my face. He had been looking at his phone, but when he senses me, he looks up, a feline grin spreading across his features.

"Alone at last, Lina."

Ugh. I cannot. "We will be on our way to Copenhagen shortly. Would you like coffee? Champagne? Something to eat?"

He cocks his head slightly, and damn, if it doesn't feel like he's reading every part of my soul. "Sit down. It's been too long since we've talked."

My jaw tightens. "I'm working."

He shrugs. "Just my luck."

The cabin phone chimes again, and I am so grateful for the interruption, I almost kiss it. Time for lift off.

CHAPTER THREE

Kasper watches me in my jump seat. I hate the designer of this plane who put the jump seat in his full view. "Is something the matter?" I ask through tight lips.

We're taxiing onto the runway.

Kasper gestures at the seat. "Why are you sitting there? The flight is empty. Sit over here." He reaches across the aisle and taps the empty chair. "Keep me company."

"It's against regulations." It isn't. There's a lot more leeway flying private.

He licks his lips again, and that traitorous part of my core that finds this alpha douche attractive kindles. "Come on, Lina. Break the rules for once. It's my plane."

I don't need his reminder that I was a "good girl" in high school, and not much has changed. "I'm here for your safety, not your whims."

He tries a different tack. "Please. I don't have anyone else to talk to, and I've already watched everything on TV."

"That's literally impossible. There are millions of hours of shows."

His mouth lifts in a lopsided smile that I hate that I find charming. "Come on, what are the odds that out of all the gin joints in the world, I stroll into yours?"

My brain wars with itself. He is the passenger. His word matters. If I do a good job, I can get hired on other flights, which will supplement my income, and I desperately need funds right now so I can figure out how to live in New York on my salary alone. Justin was good for very little, but at least he paid his half of the rent on time.

On the other hand, Kasper Frederiksen tortured me when we were at prep school together. He deserves no pity.

He gives me a pleading puppy look. No, not a puppy. A fluffy, Golden Retriever ball-of-love expression.

I hate and love it simultaneously.

"Fine," I grumble. I unlatch the seat belt and stalk the few feet to the chair across from him, my high heels sinking into the lush carpet. I'd hate to deep clean this carpet, but fortunately there's maintenance for that. "Is there anything else you need, Mr. Frederiksen?" I buckle my seatbelt across my lap. Damn him, the leather chairs are a hell of a lot more comfortable than my jumpseat.

"I'd like to know why you don't call me Kasper."

I bark a sharp laugh. "Because we were such good friends at Viceroy? This is a business arrangement, a moment in time. After we land in Copenhagen, I never have to see you again."

He frowns slightly and turns to the window. I don't regret my sharp words. I can't feign politeness all the time. It definitely didn't work with Justin.

"I thought we were friends," he says, his voice drowned by the rush of air as we lift off.

I cannot keep my incredulity at bay. All the bullshit I've dealt with over the last twenty-four hours rushes out of me. "Friends? Are you shitting me? Were we friends when you cheated off my calculus tests? When you stole my panties from my gym locker and sold them at an after-school auction? When you had sex with my best and only friend, and then ghosted her?" I cross my arms over my chest, ready for the final blow, the one that hurts me the most, but I can't do it. I can't voice it. It's the truth of my life that hangs on the edges, that I do my best not to see. The truth that I didn't deserve to go to Viceroy. I don't know how I got a scholarship, maybe because my dads lobbied for it, but I was a townie at an elite boarding school. I never fit.

And after everything with Justin, I feel like I never will, not anywhere.

He runs his hands through his hair, which would be sexy if he weren't so heinous. He exhales one long, hard breath. We've reached ten thousand feet now, cruising altitude. I should get up, and offer to make him another drink or get him something to eat. I have a checklist.

But my long-buried rage keeps my ass glued to that wicked comfortable seat.

"I'm sorry."

It's the last thing I ever expected. In high school, Kasper was the quintessential big man on campus. With his flashy European manners and supposedly panty-melting accent, he could have any girl or guy he wanted. He'd never been sorry, only smarmy, conceited. He had walked around like the reigning king he was.

Now, he apologizes. Damn me if he doesn't look sincere, too.

"I was a bit of an idiot in school," he says. "I was mad at my parents, of course. They always wanted me to be perfect, but perfect is boring." He sips his seltzer. My opinion of him must be softening, because he looks like a luxury marketing campaign, with his cobalt blue suit jacket and the steely hint of the expensive watch against his wrist. "I'm sorry about your friend. I didn't know what I wanted from sex at that age. She was very sweet, like you, too good for the likes of me."

I bite my lip. I'll bet he doesn't remember her name.

He eyes me, his gaze intense and yet sincere. "Molly, right? I heard she's getting married next year. Good for her."

My mouth goes dry, but I'm not sure why. I can't believe he remembers her name.

"Can I get you something else to drink?" I unbuckle my seatbelt and stand, holding out a hand for his empty glass.

He rolls it between his hands. How have I never noticed how long his fingers are? They look strong, too, even though they're uncalloused. He's a corporate multimillionaire, someone in charge. A brief image flashes through my mind, a hot, heated moment of imagining those fingers digging into the skin of my hips, as he thrusts into me from behind.

I shake my head to clear the thought, and fight down the flush rising on my neck. I hate Kasper Frederiksen. He doesn't deserve my dirty dreams.

I catch his gaze. His eyes are dark, like a roiling hurricane out at sea. It's doing something to me, unknitting some buttoned part of me that plays it safe.

Isn't that what Justin had said? *You're vanilla, Lina. I need spice.*

Anger at my cheating ex straightens my spine, and I take the glass out of Kasper's hands. He tilts his head, as though he's surprised.

"I'll be right back with your drink." I wheel towards the galley, but at that moment, we hit a spot of turbulence, and my heel twists in the plush carpet. My ass bumps against the side his chair, but that's not what I feel.

I glance down, as though my face moves through molasses, and stare at his hand on my hip. Liquid heat pulses from the point of our connection and pools between my legs.

I can't look at his face, but I hear the proposition in his words. It's low and steamy, and his polished accent is full of gravel. "I've got you, Lina." I could get wet just hearing his voice.

Wait. No. No, I can't. What is happening?

I pull myself away, blinking rapidly, trying to shove away all the naughty, dirty images my brain throws at me.

I hate Kasper. Molly cried for two months after Kasper broke her heart. He is a walking neon sign for Billionaire Playboy Bad Idea.

As I fix his seltzer, wishing I could crack one of the bottles of brut champagne and have a glass myself, my hands tremble. I remind myself over and over that he is bad news. I'm only fantasizing out of fatigue and reeling from the dramatic end of my two-year-relationship.

I steal a glance at him from the periphery of my vision, and my entire spine flushes. He licks his lips like he's picturing me and I'm the sweetest lollipop he's ever sucked.

My mouth fills with saliva at the thought.

Fuck, I don't talk like that. I don't think like that. I have a very long list of rules for my job, and the first five are "don't sleep with a passenger." I've seen what that kind of conduct has done to my colleagues. I can't lose my job when Justin will have the locks changed on the apartment in the three days it will take for me to get back to New York.

My hand stills as I add a sprig of rosemary to Kasper's drink. *You never take any risks,* naked, pale-ass Justin had whined. He held a pillow over his dick, like I'd ever found it impressive or distracting.

I'm taking the change in atmosphere to heart and reading into things. Kasper is interested in me.

I am many things, but I am a professional.

I clear my throat, place the crystal glass on a tray and carry it over to him, and then my resolve vanishes. His fingers drift against mine as he takes the drink, and every single place he touches ignites with desire. His gaze locks with mine, and the expression in the depths of those storm clouds adds fuel to the flames. My nipples stand to attention, straining against the fabric of my uniform. My lips part, and, fuck him, he notices. He rakes his gaze over my body, cataloguing it. My nose twitches as I catch his scent, masculine and earthy and so sensual it's difficult to breathe.

I don't know how long I withstand his scrutiny. It's like I'm naked and his eyes are his hands, caressing every part of my body. Rage and anger and dislike war inside of me, but seriously, it's fucking hot as hell. None of my ex-boyfriends have ever looked so ravenous when they looked at me. I can't breathe, and don't totally care because my long-ignored clit is throbbing and swollen.

"Sit down," he says, his voice dripping with innuendo.

I have to get control of the situation. I'm a good girl. I follow the rules. I got good grades, I please people. Sometimes, if I'm honest, to my own detriment. Sex has always been a transaction of me giving to my boyfriend, rarely getting anything in return except a "great job, babe."

Fuck that. This man here is a bona fide sex god, per all reports. There's no one else here beyond Captain Jeffers and the co-pilot, and they're behind closed doors. I've heard hate sex is mind blowing. If I can channel all of the years I've loathed Kasper Frederiksen into one orgasm, then it's one gift I can give myself during this shitty time.

"No," I say. My voice is husky, like it belongs to a different Lina. Maybe it does. Maybe it should.

His eyebrows arch and an intrigued smile tilts his lips. "No?"

"No." I lean my back against the chair opposite him, hands on my hips, jutting my chest out in my too-tight dress. Fuck, my nipples are so hard the chafing sends liquid lust straight to my core. "I'm the flight attendant. I'm the one in charge back here."

I can tell he likes that, likes the game. The foreplay. My pulse quickens but then slows. I'll never have another opportunity like this, and every girl should have mind-bending sex at least once in their lives.

"Do you like being in charge?" He sets his beautiful, artistic hands on the arm rests of his chair and flexes his pelvis slightly. I can see the outline of his cock rise against the placket of his pants.

I pull my bottom lip through my teeth, tugging gently at the flesh. "I don't know. I've never been in charge before."

"Never? What kind of idiots have you been dating?"

"Have you dated in New York? It's an island of idiots, married men, and perverts." Says the jaded recent dumpee.

"I take it of the three, you'd rather the perverts." His cock is now fully tenting his pants, and seeing his arousal only makes me wetter. I'm grateful I always listen to my dads' advice and pack extra panties.

I lick my lips, my eyes on his cock. "I've never really thought about it."

"You've never thought about kink?"

I laugh, a short, sharp bark that sounds oddly joyful. "I can't believe we're talking about kink here."

"What? With me?" A shade crosses his face but it quickly clears and there's the cocky player again. Intriguing.

"No." I settle into one hip, almost unconsciously clenching the muscles of my pussy. Friction, I need friction. "On this plane. This is my job."

His gaze is dark, a lightning storm about to happen. "So it's forbidden?" His hands tense on the chair, as though that connection is the only thing keeping him seated.

My breath hitches. Is it possible to orgasm just from talking?

Should I do this? It's wrong for many, many reasons. None of which I can remember at the moment. I don't do this, and so I want it. I want my one time.

I exhale. "Absolutely."

He runs his tongue over his lips, like he is tasting me, and it flames my entire body. "Do you want this?" He asks, his voice gruff and filled with lust. "I need to hear you say you agree."

"Agree to what?" I'm breathless, but my words are clear.

The corner of his mouth tilts upward, like he's the predator and I'm the little baby lamb. I love it. "Agree to whatever it is you want to do. I'll do anything, Lina. I'll kiss you, I'll taste you, I'll fuck you. I'll make you come so hard you'll think we're flying on angel wings of pleasure, then I'll lay you down on this buttery soft leather and make you come all over again, screaming my name and begging for more. You just have to say yes."

I know that at one point I was able to breathe. I want that. I want every single thing he asked and then I want more. "Yes."

He leaps from the chair and then his mouth is on mine, not kissing, but devouring. Plundering. His lips slant against mine, stealing my breath. Lust makes me limp, but his arms support me. He's hot, not warm, fire against my chest, the fine fabric of his shirt rubbing my too-eager nipples. He breaks the kiss for barely an instant, so we can both catch our breath, and then his mouth is on mine again, his tongue deep in my mouth. I suck on it, I bite his lip, I do the dirty things I've always wanted to do and never felt brazen enough to try. He tastes of rosemary and expensive chocolates.

He looses a deep growl from the depths of his throat, and it rumbles through my entire body, settling in my clit. Through our clothes, I rub the needy flesh against the hard length of his cock. Even through layers of fabric, my pussy simultaneously relaxes and tenses, signing for more. More.

He spears his fingers along my temples, digging into my scalp, and readjusts his position to go deeper, harder, fucking my mouth with his tongue.

"Don't mess up my hair," I say, drawing my mouth away and nipping at the curve of his neck. He groans and grinds against me when I latch onto the soft pulse point and suckle. He smells like cedar and fresh black coffee and cinnamon breakfast pastries.

"Your hair will be the least of your worries when I'm done with you." He grips my hips tightly with those long, delicious fingers of his and pulls my pelvis against his in a thrust. Sparks shoot across my vision as pleasure lights up my clit. "Fuck, Lina, you taste so good."

"I want you to know," I say, pulling up the hem of his shirt. The lean, hard planes of his stomach feel so good against my fingertips, like polished river stones. My whole body tingles with need, with anticipation. "I really hate you."

A smile flits across his face before he grabs the back of my thigh, just below to curve of my butt, and kneads it. The pain is sharp and sweet and perfect. "I can deal with that." He bends me backward in another bruising kiss, one hand kneading my ass and the other now clamped over my breast. Oh, my nipples want his mouth. They're like divining rods, waiting for attention. Stupid dress.

As if he can read my thoughts, he rolls one of them between his thumb and forefinger, the fabric pinching and grating against the sensitive skin. It feels too good, too rich, too primal. I cry out and buck my pelvis against his.

He grins as he does it again. "You like it rough, Lina?"

If this is rough, then—"Yes. Yes."

"What else do you like?" He pushes me backward into the chair and kneels between my thighs, spreading my dress tight against the skin. It's a momentary discomfort, because then he shoves my skirt up above my hips, revealing the neon purple thong I put on this morning in a fit of pique. He leans down and sniffs my pussy, and the image of this sexy, strong, rich man inhaling me sends another shock of pleasure through me.

"I like that." I'm shocked I can say anything. Most of my consciousness centers around my erogenous zones, and how every single one of them is tuned into Kasper's frequency. We've barely passed foreplay, and already I know that hate sex is addictive.

He looks up at me from between my legs, his nose still bent toward my sex. With my thong still in place, he takes a single finger and runs it down my seam. My entire body quivers, partly in anticipation, partly in desperate desire. "Tell me what else you like, Lina?"

The old, safe Lina looms in the back of my head, telling me not to be honest. Telling me to say that I like watching them come.

But I'm twenty-eight years old, and I'll never see this man again. I've hated him since high school, and maybe a part of that was because he never noticed me back then.

Besides, I'm tired of pretending. I don't care what he thinks of me.

"I like it rough," I say, my voice gravel. I let the words come from deep inside me. "Whatever you give me, I want more. I want to be so full of you that I can hardly breathe."

His eyebrow twitches, but he doesn't break. "If it's too much, you need a safe word."

Oh, goody goody. This is going to happen. I say the first word that pops into my head, no matter how illogical it is. "Avalanche."

With that, he slides the patch of fabric covering my pussy aside, and bends to devour me.

From the first clench of his lips against my clit, I buck, leaning into it, into the hot sensations of his mouth on me. He runs his teeth over the sensitive flesh, and the change in texture nearly undoes me. "Don't yet, Lina. We have a long flight. Let's make this last."

It's difficult not to come, particularly when he licks along my seam, separating my lips, then returns his focus to my clit. Each tug of his lips as he suckles me sends ripples of electric pleasure through me. I cannot keep the moan from rising, but he clamps a hand over my mouth.

I meet his gaze, "avalanche" on the tip of my tongue, but I notice he smiles, playful. Not leaving his ministrations to my sex, he nods toward the cockpit, and I get it. This is the game. Don't make noise, don't alert the captain to what we're doing.

Another flood of liquid desire gushes from me. The idea of being caught, being watched, is definitely too much, particularly when Kasper slides his fingers into me, first one, then two and three, crooking them against the inner wall of my channel. Lightning pleasure sears through me. I groan and forget to swallow it, because oh, fuck, that's where the G-spot is. I have been having stupid sex with idiots for way too long.

The orgasm erupts from me in one explosion, too fast even to feel it rise. I fuck his face through it, and I don't care. He's a big man, he can take it. I grind against his mouth and fingers as I ride out the last of the orgasm.

My body limp, I watch, my eyelids half-hooded with sleepy fog, as he kisses the juice of my arousal onto the insides of my thigh, like he's painting me with my orgasm. It's incredibly erotic, the way he licks me off his fingers, like I am a delicacy. Even though I've already come, once a rarity itself, I feel my clit prickle with renewed awareness. *What happens now?*

Kasper stands, a sexy half-smile crossing his handsome face, making him even better looking, the dick. His hands go to the waistband of his trousers, his fingertips resting on the zipper. Yes, that is my clit throbbing again, wanting to know what he is going to do. "Are you still in charge, Lina?"

I'm foggy and sparking and I can't believe we are both still clothed. It's a massive problem. I hook my fingers into the waistband of his trousers and yank him toward me.

"Tell me what you're thinking." He runs his fingers through my hair, sifting the strands like he's weaving them, and it's so sensual, warmth blooms in my chest.

I don't like the warmth. This is hate sex, nothing more. Right?

So I take control. "I'm thinking that I want your cock. I want to taste it, and then I want you to fuck me so hard my toes curl and I bite the chair to keep from screaming."

He holds onto the pseudo-tender moment for another instant, then lets me unzip him. He's wearing silky black boxer shorts, and without the zipper blocking it, his dick swells until the smooth tip protrudes from the fabric. My mouth waters. I've never loved sucking cock, but for some reason I can't process currently, I want this one.

I pull down his boxers and wrap a firm hand around his base. He leans back, moaning, pumping into my hand.

This is control. I have him right where I want him. Or, I will.

I keep my eyes on his face as I run my tongue from the base of his hard, thick cock all the way to the smooth, rubbery tip. There's a milky drip of pre-come collecting along the slit, and I lick it, burrowing my tongue into him the way he did me. He thrusts his cock past my lips but I pull back. "Naughty, naughty," I say. Who am I?

I don't care. I like this Lina.

He meets my gaze and runs his tongue along his lips.

"You'll suck it soon enough. Right now I just want to fuck that hot, sweet pussy. You dripped all over me, and I've been throbbing ever since, thinking about the way you'll clench around me."

I don't hesitate. "Yes."

He takes a foil condom packet out of his back pocket, because of course this player keeps one there at all times. I have to remember that. This is something he does, all the time. I'm another conquest to him.

I don't care. This is the most fun I've ever had and I want more.

"On your knees," he growls. He takes me by the hips and flips me over in the chair, so my arms wrap around the head-rest. I press my swollen, aching nipples against the cushion, and damn, the pressure feels so good. Even though I've already come, my clit and pussy are desperate for more.

He pushes my dress up above my ass again, then runs an appreciative hand over the curves of my flesh. "So pretty." He runs a finger down the valley between the globes, pausing over the pucker of skin. "Has anyone ever touched you here?"

"I'm not ready for that." Though now that he mentions it, I've always been a little curious.

"All right." He grips my hips with his hands and I feel his weight shift behind me. I glance down, and holy fuck, it's better than I imagined, seeing the long lines of his fingers wrap around my skin. He lines his cock up with the seam of my sex, and draws it back and forth, teasing me, applying just enough pressure to make me want more. "You're dripping, Lina. I need to be good and soaked to fuck you hard. You're such a good girl, you can take it. Do you want it?"

"Yes." I whimper, the slight pressure against my clit an itch demanding to be scratched. "I want it. I want that cock."

He leans over my shoulder, and I drown in the heady scent of him. How does a man smell this good? He kisses the side of my neck, the lobe of my ear, and I feel the tip of his cock notch at my entrance. "When I fuck you, Lina, I want you to say my name."

"Yes." My word is barely a breath. My whole body is alive, tingling in anticipation.

"Say it." He thrusts into me, spreading my walls wide, and sensation blooms throughout my whole body. It feels un-fucking-believable. He pulls my thighs further apart and thrusts again, so hard he strikes the sparking bundle of nerves that is my G-spot. I cry out, and he clenches my skin, a reminder to stay quiet. Fuck, it is too hot. "Say my name."

"Kasper," I whisper.

He strokes into me again, and again, and again, each thrust going deeper, stretching me wider, filling me until this is my whole world, everything I have ever wanted. Every time the tip of his dick hits my G-spot, I shudder, the plea-sure overwhelming, like a fever of want.

Vanilla, my ass.

"Say it," he repeats.

"Kasper. Kasper." Each time I plead, I am rewarded with more sensation, more of him. I clench the walls of my pussy around him, searching for more, more. The elusive second orgasm is now crashingly close.

"Fuck, Lina, you are perfect." He grunts and picks up the rhythm. "Can I keep going?"

"Don't you fucking stop," I manage.

I push back against him when he thrusts, the flesh of my ass slapping into his lower belly. I feel it in his pace, how he likes that. He's losing control, and so am I, and for once I don't care. I lean forward as pleasure tears through me, biting hard on the leather seat I'm clutching for dear life. How has he found my G-spot so easily? None of my other boyfriends ever got close. I see the ridge of pleasure just in front of me, and I chase it, matching him stroke for stroke, slamming down on his dick as he is balls deep inside of me, letting the rocketing sensation propel me forward. The cabin fills with the slap of wet, hot flesh against flesh.

Then he shifts the position of one of his hands, rubbing his thumb in circles over my clit, and I break.

"Kas!" I cry. I clench around him in my ecstasy, milking him, and he comes undone with me. I feel the tight pool of lust coiling in his lower spine as he pushes into me again and again, filling the condom with his sticky, hot semen.

I can't breathe, can't move. The pleasure recedes from my body like adrenaline, leaving me quivery and cool, but my muscles feel limp and sated.

Kasper collapses against me, his chest to my back, his dick still inside of me. "You are fucking amazing."

Confusing warmth blossoms through me again. That was everything I had ever dreamed of and far more. Addictive, almost.

In my fog, I realize I need to control the situation again. This is Kasper, destroyer of prep school dreams. Okay, he's also Kasper, the sex king, but this was a one-time deal.

It also dawns on me that I'm at work on this private jet with a captain who can fire me for impropriety, and my thighs are sticky from sex, I have no idea where my thong went, and I currently have my passenger's dick still inside of me. Impossibly, it's getting hard again.

I pull myself away from him and stand in the aisle on shaking legs.

Kasper lies back in the chair and sighs. "Rats. Good girl Lina is back." He pouts, then takes a tissue from his pocket and wraps the used condom in it. "Don't worry. I own the plane. It's not like you're getting fired."

Oh my God, I can't breathe. This isn't happening. I need to find control again.

So I do the only logical thing. I run to the bathroom.

CHAPTER 4

My face doesn't belong to me. My makeup is smudged, my hair hangs wild, pins askew. My cheeks are flushed and my lips are swollen.

I absolutely look like I've been fucked, and fucked well.

A smile tilts one corner of my mouth. All right, yes, Kasper was an immature party dick in high school. But high school is over, and the sex was amazing with a capital A and three exclamation marks.

I don't have to see him again. I only have to make it through the rest of this flight. As soon as we land, I'll text Sarah and ream her out for not warning me about Kasper, but I don't have to fly this line any longer. I have my regular, commercial route, and I can find another private moonlighting gig.

No one has to know I just fucked my passenger while on the job. Twice, technically.

This is fine. I am still me.

I pee and use the Egyptian cotton towels in the bathroom to clean the sticky residue of sex from my legs. Still no idea where my panties are, but I can get a pair from my suitcase. I fix my makeup, going for a cleaner, fresher look this time. A look that says "no, I absolutely did not break the cardinal rule of my profession."

I've lost too many hair pins to fix my French twist, but I have a spare rubber band on my wrist, so I pull my waves up into a neat ponytail.

There. Now I only half-look like I've just been railed by my prep school nemesis.

I smile at my reflection and leave the bathroom, straightening my dress.

Kasper stands in front of the bathroom, looking incredibly sexy with his disheveled light brown hair and untucked shirt. He's taken off his suit jacket, and the entire look, from his partially-unbuttoned collar to the relaxed jut of his hip against the wall of the cabin, makes him look like a fucking magazine model.

My body tingles again, but I shrug it off. *Once and done. Once and done.* "Did you need something, Mr. Frederiksen?"

A smirk plays around his swollen lips. "I need you to call me Kasper. We can keep Mr. Frederiksen for role play."

A swirl of heat eddies around my low spine. "That's not happening." I push past him, and to his credit, he lets me go. I busy myself with one of the compartments reserved for crew luggage. I pull another pair of panties from my suitcase and stuff them into my pocket. I'll put them on later, when he's not paying attention.

I turn back to him. I'm me again. Lina.

He's sitting in his chair again, scrolling through his phone with his thumb. He glances up as I slide into the jump seat with my e-reader.

He puts the phone down and sighs loudly. "Lina."

I hate that I like how he says my name, like he's been waiting to say it for ages. "Yes?"

"Sit with me."

"No." I swipe my e-reader to open the book I've been reading but the words dance and swirl in front of me. Damn two orgasms, making me all distracted.

"Please?" Even without looking at him, I know he's pleading.

"You're like a three-year-old." A smile tugs at my lips and I force my mouth into a thin, professional line.

"I'm bored. You're sitting right there. Come and talk to me."

"I'm working."

"No, you're reading. Please, Lina?"

I see it now, the charm that other girls saw in high school. The pretty, sexy rich boy into games. Maybe he's one of those men who can't bear to be alone.

I don't know why I'm spending this much time thinking about him. He always made it abundantly clear that little townie Lina wasn't worth his time in high school.

Though our activities over the last hour indicate that may have changed.

No, he's just a fling. A one-time way to work out my sexual needs, for once in my entire life.

I'm not vanilla. Fuck you, Justin, and your stupid sex tape. What I just did with Kasper? It would have broken the internet.

His eyes bore into me, as though he can read my thoughts. I desperately hope he can't. "Want to talk about it, Lina?"

"No." I wish I had a paperback instead of an e-book so I can slam it closed. "Would you care to see the menu? I should start on lunch if you're hungry."

"Not for lunch." He waggles his eyebrows in a faux seductive manner, and it's so unexpectedly endearing, I can't hold back the bark of laughter that escapes. "See? I can make you smile."

"I don't know why you want to."

"You don't want to attribute it to boredom?"

"You must always be bored, then."

"You have no idea." He yawned, his eye twinkling. "Besides, this is fun. You're fun."

Warmth blooms down my spine. I could sit next to him. There's still hours left in the flight. Maybe it's that he gave me two orgasms more than any of my previous boyfriends, but I think he might be kind of cute.

I stand and move towards the chair. Not the one we had sex in, because I need to clean that shortly.

He grins at me, his handsome face creasing. "So, how are you a flight attendant?"

Ah, there it is. I should have known. You can never just have sex with the guy you hate, you have to listen to him talk, which ruins everything.

"I don't need your validation for my life choices," I say, calculating how long I need to sit here. Maybe the captain will let me sit in the extra seat in the cockpit.

Of course, he doesn't see anything wrong with his question. His casual elitism blinds him to anything other than him and his lifestyle.

"I don't know anyone else from Viceroy who—"

"Who what?" I know my tone is strident, but seriously. "Works in a service industry? I love what I do. I would hate being cooped up all day in an office, working my ass off for some entitled asshole. I pick my shifts. I travel the world. I use my language skills."

His eyes widen and he runs his tongue between his lips, as though he likes that I'm disagreeing with him. My pussy clenches, as though it feels the sparks his gaze shoots at me.

"You don't want to be in charge?"

"If I got promoted, I wouldn't be able to fly as much. I'd be in meetings or stuck on the ground. No, thank you."

Maybe one day. One day if I find the right person and can settle down. Otherwise, my wanderlust both rules my life and excuses it.

"So, you think I'm an entitled rich guy? That's all I am to you?"

I laugh despite myself. "And you think I'm some poor little townie, who got in to Viceroy on a pity scholarship. Barely good enough to breathe the same air as you. Right?"

His body freezes, and his brow furrows. "I don't think that at all. You're the smartest person I've ever met, Lina. Maybe you need to re-examine your impostor syndrome."

The compliment settles somewhere between my breasts and my abdomen.

He nestles into his chair and closes his eyes. The prince asleep. "Unless you'd like to fuck again, which I'll be up for in about ten minutes, I might sleep for a bit. Real conversations are so damned exhausting. Would you dim the cabin lights?"

I stand, as though moving through a cave of ice and do as he asked.

I had sex with Kasper Frederiksen, and then he called me the smartest person he's ever met.

The world is one messed up, topsy turvy place.

* * *

HE SLEEPS the remainder of the flight, thank goodness. I can't process what happened, and I don't really want to do so. Instead, I focus on my job, my e-book, and whatever the captain and co-pilot need.

I wake him shortly before we start our descent. "Kasper, we're almost in Copenhagen."

His eyes blink open slowly, the hints of gray in them hot and dark, like he's been having some very naughty dreams. The half-tent in his pants testifies to that, too, but I am almost out of this awkward situation, and I just want to finish this flight and log the memories into my spank bank for later. Maybe I'll finally buy a vibrator, if I can ever decide which one to try.

He tilts his neck to either side, his sleep-filled gaze locked on mine, heat behind those stormy eyes. "Time for my seat to go in its full and upright position?"

"Like I haven't heard that before." I hand him a freshly made cup of coffee, made to his specifications per the dossier Sarah gave me. She told me how he takes his coffee, but didn't see fit to tell me who he was. Oh, Sarah.

"Don't sit in the jumpseat. Sit next to me." He sips at the coffee. He's pretty cute when he's waking up, not that I want to linger here with him. Hate sex should not involve watching someone else wake up. It's too intimate.

I take the seat across the aisle from him, smelling of the cleanser I used on it earlier. It's a good reminder of my earlier resolution. Once we land, I'm out of here. He doesn't need to know more about me.

"Is this your first time in Copenhagen?" he asks.

"Maybe."

"You know, when you don't directly answer a question, it doesn't make you mysterious. It just makes you sound like a bitch." He says it playfully, like he knows that riling me gets me hot. He shouldn't know that. Thank fuck this was a one-time thing.

"I am a bitch. Didn't you know?" I grin sweetly at him, but the expression he returns is so full of heat and lust that I can't bear it for more than a second. I turn my gaze out the window. It's daytime here. We flew through the night and across the ocean, and here we are. Damn it, I love flying.

"Where are you staying?" he asks.

"I don't know yet. Why?"

"Because I have a house where you could stay if you were so inclined."

That's unexpected. I sneak a peek at him. He's staring down at his coffee cup, swirling it slowly. "You want me to stay at your house?"

"If you'd like. It's just sitting there. Besides, it would make it easier for when you decide you want to have sex with me again."

"Hah." Though would that be the worst thing? Yes. I'm already softening in my opinion of him. I don't need to waste more time indulging in that line of thinking.

He leaves it a beat, then says, "Why don't you know where you're staying? The Lina I remember would have planned every single aspect of the trip beforehand."

I tuck my ponytail back behind my shoulder. "Maybe I'm more spontaneous now."

"I like spontaneous Lina. She's dead sexy."

My cheeks flush, and I look away from him. I don't want him to like me. Do I? No. No. I ponder a response, but the urge to be honest is overwhelming. Maybe because I don't really care what he thinks of me. "Sometimes, when I go to a new city, I don't make any plans. I walk around for hours, trying to find the part of town that speaks to me. Then I look for a place to stay around there, the best I can afford."

"Sounds like a good way to explore a city."

I stare out the window at the clouds beyond. "I've found some great places that way. A flat in Vienna overlooking the Danube. A hotel in Los Angeles set deep in the hills. A rental in Bangkok overlooking the Rama VIII Bridge."

His gaze on the back of my neck is hot and loaded. "You've been everywhere."

"Not everywhere." I turn and tilt a half-smile at him. "I've never been to Copenhagen."

His expression is oddly sober, earnest. "Stay with me. You

can meet my best friend and business partner, Mads. You'll like him. He's very serious."

"No, thanks." So what if it's tempting? I don't need more indulgence. I need to process my break up grief, not spend more time with Kasper and his enigmatic serious friend.

"Really. There's no one better to take you for fermented shark."

I guffaw. "Fermented shark?"

"You've never heard of our famous Danish fermented shark? What kind of traveler are you?" Ah, here he is again. The playful childlike Kasper.

"It sounds revolting."

His eyes spark. "It is. You could call it an acquired taste."

I smile. "I'll pass."

"That's wise." He holds my gaze for a moment. "Give me your number."

The plane wheels whir as they lower. Captain Jeffers announces overhead that we're almost there. The sound in the cabin is a deafening roar and screech.

I'm grateful it gives me a moment. "Why?"

"Because then you'll have it when you decide you're tired of traipsing around the city on your own." He drains his coffee. "Or if you want to have sex again. Who knows? Maybe you'll like Mads, too."

The sound of the plane landing drowns out my laughter.

CHAPTER 5

He tries to convince me again to go with him, but I hold my stance. One time sex. That's all I needed. Did I also discover that maybe I like Kasper more than I thought? I don't know, but I refuse to give it more mental energy.

As I tidy the plane, I scour it, looking for my panties. Nowhere. *Shit.* I doubt it will be the first time the cleaning crew finds a random thong. Which is what I need to remember. Kasper is a player. He just wants his dick touched. He doesn't want more from me, and I don't want anything more from him.

Exactly.

I follow the copilot and Captain Jeffers from the terminal. She's already on her phone, calling her wife to let her know we've arrived safely. "You did a good job, Lina. I hope we'll meet again." She shakes my hand and heads off towards a waiting car service.

A twinge of guilt twists in my chest. A good job? Joining the Mile High club at work is not my idea of a job well done.

I follow the signs towards the train station, moving at a

brisk pace in my heels. Once I get to the city center, I'll find a cafe, have a pasty and a coffee, and search for places to go and things to see. I can't let last night's…activities faze me.

I had incredible hate sex with Kasper Frederiksen, but that's over, and I need to move on with my life.

Once I get a seat on the train, I turn my phone off airplane mode and my international plan flashes a warning. It's fine. It's a luxury I need. I fire off a *WTF* text to Sarah. It's the middle of the night in New York, so she won't get it for a few hours, but it makes me feel better to have sent it.

My phone rings as I'm about to stow it back in my purse. My stomach plummets, but I answer anyway, sticking in my ear buds so the surrounding passengers can't eavesdrop.

"Hi, Dad. What are you doing up so late?"

My father Kenneth pops up on the video call screen. "Hi, peanut! Just missing you. Where are you?"

"What?" My other dad, Rafael, looms over Kenneth's shoulder. Whereas Kenneth has short-cropped light hair, Rafael's hair is full and black, streaked with an attractive amount of gray at the temples. They both grin at me, their smiles broad and hopeful. "What does he mean? I thought you were going to be on the ground for a while. We were going to see if you and Justin wanted to come up and visit."

My dads are the two most wonderful people in the entire world. That doesn't mean I love spilling the sordid details of my fresh breakup with them.

"Um, I'm in Copenhagen." If I hedge long enough, maybe I will find some excuse. "I had to get out of town."

"Why?" Rafael says. He then disappears, then re-appears in his own screen a moment later, so there's a triptych of me, him, and Kenneth on my phone screen. Uh oh. That means he knows it's serious, if he doesn't want to spy over Kenneth's shoulder. "Lina, tell us what's going on."

"Rafael." Kenneth's hand appears on his shoulder. "Don't pry. We promised we wouldn't pry into her life. Remember?"

"Yes, but—"

"Dad, it's okay. Really."

Oh fuck, they're both staring at me earnestly. I can practically see their wide-eyed pleading even though I'm thousands of miles away. "Justin and I broke up yesterday. So I took a flight to Copenhagen." I show them the sights flickering by out of my window. "See? It's beautiful. It's practically all water."

"That's because you're a water sign," Rafael says, his voice heavily laden with affection. "You're always happiest near water or in the air."

"Wouldn't that make me an air sign?" He knows full well I don't believe in astrology. I just love teasing him. Besides, it draws the attention from me.

"Lina, why don't you come home? We can heal your broken heart here." My dads have wanted me to move closer to home for the past five years. They accepted for a while that because of my job, I need to be by the airport, but the older I get, the more they pester. In an endearing way.

"I'm fine. All right? I love it here already." If I talk to them for much longer, I'm going to cry. This is how it always goes after I break up with someone.

"Where are you staying?"

"With a friend." My eyes widen in the reflection on the screen. Shit. I hadn't meant to say that, to lie to them. My dads hate when I wing it in a city. I don't want to worry them, but now they're going to ask—

"Which friend?"

I cannot lie to them again. Maybe one of them, but both, at the same time? It's a horrible weakness of mine. "Kasper Frederiksen." My voice sounds like a mouse's squeak. Good girl Lina, afraid of disappointing her dads.

To my surprise, they grin. "That super cute guy from high school who had such a thing for you?" Rafael asks.

"Rafael, we agreed we wouldn't tell her that."

"But, Kenneth—"

I hold up my hand. "He did not have a thing for me in high school. He was heinous to me in high school."

"He was probably just jealous that you're so much smarter than he is." Aww, Dad.

"I don't think that was it," I reply.

"Honey," Kenneth says, his handsome, craggy face very serious. "If you're going to have a fling to get back at Justin, make sure you take care of yourself."

I roll my eyes, even as my stomach churns a little. "That's not going to happen. I always take care of myself."

"We know, *carina*," Rafael says. "There's nothing wrong with letting someone else take care of you, too."

Tears prickle at the backs of my eyes. I have no idea why. "I love you both. My train is pulling into the station. I'll call you soon."

"Have fun, sweet pea."

The call ends and I stow my phone as I stare out the window. It's a beautiful morning, the kind of sunny that enriches colors rather than washes them out. It's clean and fresh and bright, and all it does is remind me that I have no idea what I'm doing.

CHAPTER 6

*A*fter a delicious and restorative breakfast of coffee and pastry, my feet itch to explore. I change in the cafe's restroom, out of my defiled uniform and into a pair of gray wool slacks and low-heeled boots.

I stroll along the waterfront in the new port, admiring the colorful, narrow buildings. The outdoor cafes are already set up and waiting under green and white awnings. More bicycles than I have ever seen crowd along the wide shoulders of the boulevard. The air smells of brine and baking and coffee.

Normally, I love this aimlessness. I have nowhere to be, no one expecting me, nothing desired from me.

Except I can't stop thinking about Kasper. I remember his hands on my hips, his tongue in my mouth. Coffee both helps and harms, because it reminds me of him.

My phone pings. Sarah must have woken up.

Sorry, not sorry ;) Was he that smoking in high school???

I smile despite myself.

Not the point.

...

And yes.

She sends back a gif of a squealing actress.

He's not my type.

She replies with, *why? Because he didn't post a sex tape of him and some other woman online?*

Aaaargh. She knows me too well. Fucking Justin.

Whatever, I type. I smell a coffee stall, and the lure is too great. I continue texting as I wait in line. The scent makes it almost so I can taste him again.

Have fun in DK, Sarah writes. *Going back to bed. See you in three days!!!* She adds several kissy face emojis.

I slide my phone into the pocket of my slacks, and order my coffee. Fuck me, I can smell Kasper's cologne. Maybe I should hightail it out of Copenhagen and head straight for Stockholm, because my mind is clearly playing tricks on me.

I turn around, take-out cup in hand, and nearly spill my drink all over myself.

"You look like a Dane already, Lina." Kasper grins broadly and one of his eyebrows twitches upward.

Fuck me. Behind him stands one of the most handsome men I've ever seen. He's tall with pale skin, dark hair, shadowy features, and he looks like the star of a teenaged vampire show. My mouth goes dry, and, not knowing what else to do, I paste on an insipid expression.

"Kasper? What are you doing here?" Not my best effort, but at least I didn't drool over his friend.

Kasper has his hands in the pockets of his suit pants. He's changed since the flight, and now he's wearing dark gray suit that makes his eyes look almost teal. I search them for the little bits of gray, but it makes me lightheaded. He looks good enough to eat. "We had a business meeting, and thought we'd get something to eat. This is my friend, Mads. Mads, this is Lina."

Mads leans into me and kisses both cheeks quickly. He

smells so good, like cotton and sandalwood and spice, my knees go weak. "Charmed, Lina. I've heard a lot about you."

"Really?" Why on earth would Kasper be talking about me? "I promise, none of it's true."

A mischievous smile plays across Mads's lips. "I hope that's not accurate."

My pulse skyrockets. Did Kasper tell him that we'd had sex on the plane? Not knowing what else to do, I sip my coffee and nearly burn myself.

"Where is your suitcase?" Kasper asks. "Did you find your perfect place to stay already?"

"No. I left it in a locker at the train station. I'll get it later."

"Hmm." Kasper rocks back and forth on his heels. "Have you decided to come and stay with me?"

"Hah. No." Though a rush of heat races down my spine at the look these two are giving me.

"Why don't you join us for a meal?" Mads asks. His voice is smooth and creamy, like a cup of hot cocoa on a frigid winter's day. I'm clearly delirious if I'm being so prosaic.

I bite my lip and look around, as though a solution will present itself. Why am I fighting this? Even if Kasper was a douche in high school, he's been fairly civil. Mads is gorgeous and sophisticated. They're locals. They would just be showing me around a town where I'm a stranger.

"All right."

CHAPTER 7

We walk to a cafe not far from the port. Kasper and Mads talk between themselves, their voices low and conspiratorial. It doesn't bother me. I take in the sights of the city. Copenhagen is gorgeous, an intriguing mix of medieval and new Scandinavian.

After we are seated with our menus in hand, Mads turns his wattage towards me. I glow a little in his limelight. I've never sat beside two such incredible men before.

No wonder the waitress is still ogling our table.

"Lina, tell me about yourself," Mads says.

That's an opening line for the ages. How to begin? *Yes, I lost my Mile High Club cherry to your friend sitting right there?* No, probably better to keep sex out of it, though my lady parts are decidedly aware of these men.

"I'm from a small town in the Berkshires," I say. "It's not home to much of note. Some orchards, art galleries, and Viceroy."

"The boarding school where you met Kasper?" Mads asks, and I nod.

Our waitress arrives and we order, a selection of smorrebrod, a local specialty of open-faced sandwiches. When I choose the herring, Kasper insists as well on a round of aquavit. I decide to roll with it. It's easier thinking about food than high school.

"What was Kasper like in school?" Mads asks.

I glance at Kasper, whose expression is nonchalant. I measure my words. "I don't think I'm the best person to answer that. He graduated two years before I did. Where did the two of you meet?" Deflection is better, but I feel Kasper's gaze on me, like he knows I am holding back. I sip my water to calm my nerves.

"Mads and I are old family friends," Kasper answers. "We realized we have… similar tastes."

"And now you work together?" I ask.

"Yes."

The waitress brings a round of drinks, beer for them and a white wine for me, along with the flutes of aquavit.

I sip my wine. It's sweet and light, especially after all the coffee I've had. "What kind of work do you do?"

Mads answers with a throwaway gesture. "We own clubs, members only, exclusive. High class."

"So not the kind of places I'd be welcome?" I mean it as a joke, but both men frown slightly, their faces closing.

"You would be more than welcome," Kasper says. There's something in his expression I cannot read, something full of yearning and lust. It thrills me, this pseudo-invitation. I know it shouldn't.

I'm saved needing to reply by the arrival of our food. Thick slices of Danish rye bread filled with seeds and topped with smoked fish and a lovely rainbow of herbs and toppings. Yum.

The two men are both eyeing me intently, and maybe the jet lag is catching up to me or the wine has gone straight to my head, but lust curls in my belly and fogs my brain. All I can think of is filling my stomach and then convincing one or both of these men to fuck me in the bathroom. The very thought of four hands on my body is enough to make me perspire with want.

Which is completely inappropriate. The thing with Kasper was one time, and I met Mads barely five minutes ago.

Space. I need space to get my head back in the game. I push back from the table, rattling the silverware. "I'm going to the ladies' room."

I head for the rear of the restaurant where there's a small white door. I enter the restroom, but as I'm closing the door, a heavy, male hand with long, beautiful fingers holds it open.

"Can I come in, Lina?" Kasper asks, a wicked grin slanting across his face.

My heart rate enters hyper speed. My cheeks flush. *No.* I should say no. I should put a stop to this wild attraction. "Yes," I say.

In moments, his mouth and body are pressed against mine. He spins me and pushes me back against the door, closing it with a hearty thud. There's so much need in this kiss, so much pent-up desire, that it's hard to breathe.

I don't entirely want to.

I ball my hands in the silky lapels of his shirt and pull him closer. I thrust my tongue past his teeth, tasting him. A moan coils in my throat and I press it into his mouth. This kiss, this need, goes straight to my clit, making it throb a burning red. Wanting friction, I rub my pelvis against his. There's too much fabric in the way.

"I'm glad we found you." He nips at the tender skin beneath my ear, and pulls something silky from the pocket of his suit pants. "Want these back?"

He dangles my thong, the one I thought I'd lost on the plane, in front of my face. It's still wet, and smells of sex and

Kasper. Heat coils deep in my core, and I moan, licking my lips.

"This is mine now. I'm going to keep it and wrap it around my cock when I jerk off, thinking about your sweet, hot pussy." He stuffs the thong back into his pocket, his weight still against me. I love it. Beneath him, I feel secure, desired. "Do you want to be mine, too?"

I bite my lip as he grinds his thick cock against the angle between my thighs again. Pressure, more pressure. "I want things on my terms." He liked this game before.

He spins me around, and I brace myself against the door with my palms. "Are you a good girl, Lina?" He cups my breasts through my sweater, tweaking the taut nipples. I bite my lip to hold back the cry of pleasure. "Tell me what you want."

I grind my ass against his hardened cock, but he stills me with a hand on my hip. "You have to say it, Lina." I wiggle and writhe but he holds me fast.

This is the game. I want it so badly, I can feel it pulsing through my veins. Between panting breaths, I say, "I want you to fuck me, Kasper."

He presses a kiss to the base of my neck and runs his tongue from my shoulder up to my ear, catching my lobe between his teeth. It's light and teasing and so fucking hot, I need a new pair of panties. Arousal drips down my inner thigh.

"Please," I say, my voice thin.

He moves one hand to the placket of my gray slacks and pulls down the zipper. With his other hand, he circles my nipple with his long, succulent fingers. "You like this, Lina?" He slides his hand down my lower belly, past the hem of my simple cotton underwear. He cups my sex and hisses in my ear. "So perfect, so wet. You are so beautiful, Lina."

He's so close to my clit and yet so far away. I rub myself against his hand, desperate, mad with need.

He complies, sliding one finger between my wet seam, spreading my lips wide, before settling his palm directly atop the sensitive bundle of nerves. Fireworks shoot behind my eyes as I groan.

He pumps his cock against my ass. "You like this, Lina? You like getting fucked in a restaurant? Where anyone could walk in? Where anyone could hear you?"

"Yes." I can't even lie. Between my nipples and my pussy, he has me completely whipped. I'd do or say anything to finish this.

"Good girl." He slaps my clit lightly with his fingers, and the combination of pain and pleasure is so intense, I almost climax. But then he slides two fingers inside me and it's just enough of a shift to extend the wave of pleasure.

He rocks his erection against my ass as my orgasm builds inside of me. I've never come this quickly, not even while masturbating.

His breath is hot against my neck, sticky and sexy and smelling of hops and barley and coffee. "You like it when I fuck you? Say my name, Lina."

"Kasper." It's almost a hiss, because I am so close. He throbs his palm against my clit while his fingers pulse inside of me. I clench around them. Yes. Yes.

"Do you like Mads, Lina?"

This is a left turn, but I don't mind because I am so close, so very, very close. "Yes."

"Do you think he'd like it, watching your face as I fuck you?"

Oh. Wait, is that a possibility? The cresting of pleasure slows, but he tweaks my nipple, sending shivers down my lower spine and pooling in my already soaking pussy.

"Or do you want me to watch you ride his hard, thick

cock? I'd love to see that, to see that pretty pussy of yours wrapped around him."

"Yes." I lean my head against him, rubbing my clit harder against his palm. That idea, of being watched, turns me on so much my whole body feels like it's on fire.

"Say you'll come home with me," Kasper whispers.

I'm so close, so close, and he holds my orgasm a finger's breadth away, the bastard. "Please," I manage.

"Say you'll come home with me. Say my name."

I want the release so badly, so very badly. And after this, why am I saying no to going to his house? Why don't I let myself have some fun for once? "Yes. Yes, Kas, yes. Please, please."

He fucks me harder, ramming his fingers into me, strumming my G-spot like a guitar and I break all at once, the orgasm gushing from me. I spasm around his hand, pulling his fingers deeper, and he holds me through it all, stroking every highly sensitized part.

As the pleasure ebbs, Kasper removes his hands from me. I turn, panting, cheeks flushed, hair mussed, and watch with a watering mouth as he pumps his thick cock. It's incredibly satisfying, watching him pleasure himself, watching his face contort until he shoots his semen into the toilet with a grunt. He likes that I watch him, his gaze locked with mine as he gets himself off.

He breathes heavily, as he tucks himself back into his slacks. I haven't moved from my spot by the door. I watch through heavy-lidded eyes as he gets a towel, wets it, and moves towards me. With a gentle touch, he swipes the moist towel across my forehead, my cheeks, underneath my eyes, washing me clean. He gets a new towel and applies it to my pussy, the coolness unbelievably soothing against my hot, aroused flesh.

He dries me, then zips my slacks and presses a soft kiss to my forehead. "Let's have lunch, and then we'll head home."

After he leaves, I collapse on the toilet in a boneless, satisfied heap. What have I gotten myself into? Whatever it is, I'm kind of looking forward to it.

CHAPTER 8

$\mathcal{O}$f course, in a city of bicycle transportation, they have a sleek black car service. We cruise through the streets. The buildings remind me of a combination of Stockholm and Vienna, a mixture of Renaissance and Baroque and Romantic architecture. Lots of windows and narrow buildings and winding roads with enormous bike lanes. No wonder it's voted one of the most livable and expensive cities in the world.

Mads sits beside me, and catches my gaze. "Copenhagen is renowned for our green spaces. We will take you. The King's Gardens around Rosenborg castle are particularly lovely."

He has soft hazel eyes that ooze intelligence and charm. I can't help but remember Kasper's words in the bathroom. What would it feel like to have those hazel eyes on me? I wonder if he's thought about it. I wonder if he knows Kasper fucked me in the bathroom.

I like wondering about it.

"That would be wonderful. I've always found a good long walk to help with jet lag."

Kasper laughs. He's unbuttoned the top of his shirt, revealing an inch of skin. I have never found collarbones sexy before, but damn, his are nice. I could trace the whole length with my tongue and never get bored.

I snap my eyes back to the scenery flicking by. I'm letting my long-dormant libido get the better of me.

"Where do you live?" I ask.

Mads answers as Kasper frowns at a message on his phone. "Frederiksberg. It's a nice area, lots of cafes, restaurants, shopping."

"That sounds great." I should have brought nicer lingerie with me. In my defense, I have never needed it before on one of my trips. Maybe I can buy more. Though the longer I stare at these two men, the less I want to wear.

Kasper sighs at Mads, sliding his phone back into his pocket. "It's a shitshow at the club. I'll have to head over after we drop off Lina. Unless you want to take care of the business?" He waggles his eyes, but there's a hard ruthlessness in his expression.

Mads shrugs, and I feel the heat of his gaze on the back of my neck. My entire spine tingles. "I think Lina and I can manage."

Yeah. If a person could orgasm by voice alone, Mads's would get me every time. He should narrate romance novels.

The driver turns the car into a neighborhood full of wide, tree-lined boulevards, stately homes and apartments that are more works of art than living spaces. It's May, so the sidewalk cafes are filled with people.

Mads leans over me, pointing at a sign and engulfing me in his sweet, smoky scent. "The zoo is over that way. It's very popular with the families." I close my eyes and inhale, memorizing his scent.

When I open my eyes, we are parked in front of a

wrought iron gate that opens like the start of a haunted mansion movie.

Holy fuck, it *is* a mansion.

The short driveway rolls past a trim, minimalist landscape, but the house is the real stunner. It's at least three stories, Romantic at its heart, all white with black trim and shutters. There are too many windows to count.

"You live *here?*" I ask as the driver parks the car then gets out, moving toward the trunk. "How does a place like this even exist in this city?"

Kasper shrugs in his manor-bred way. "It's a family house. My parents moved to Charlottenlund a few years ago, so I live here now." He nods towards Mads. "Mads, too."

Mads turns his aristocratic charm towards me. "What can I say? He took in a lonely kid."

Kasper rolls his eyes and steps from the car like he's about to walk a red carpet. "No one buys the poor little rich boy act, Mads."

I'm glued to my seat, my gaze fixed on this impossible homestead. At Viceroy, I knew Kasper came from wealth. It was obvious to anything with a pulse that he was rich, as were most of our classmates. But this, in the middle of a chic European city, is a level of wealth I cannot fathom.

Mads stands beside my open car door, his hand extended. Up close, his fingernails have a better manicure than mine. I'm not surprised.

I take his proffered hand, and the skin is warm and smooth in mine. His touch reassures me. I belong here. I was invited. They want me here.

That realization heats my core all by itself.

I climb out of the car, and the house looks even larger than it did from inside the vehicle.

Mads loops my hand through the crook of his arm, which

feels so impossibly good I almost swoon. This is not off to an auspicious start.

I gasp when we enter the home. The entryway boasts forty-foot high ceilings with a white petaled chandelier illuminating everything with soft, warm light. There are cozy knit and fleece blankets on every surface.

I remove my shoes, stowing them in one of the little bins beside the door. Mads takes my light coat and hangs it on one of the iron S-hooks.

My eyes flit around the open floorplan. Neutral, cozy-looking Scandinavian furniture amid glass and beiges and grays. I can see to the dining room, dominated by a massive hand-carved wooden table and a glass chandelier that looks as though it's been hung with crystal piano keys.

"You guys really like candles." I touch the designer candle nearest me, as this seems the safest thing to say. It's certainly not a sex dungeon, as I may or not may not have been mentally entertaining. It's a home. Cozy, warm, full of life and history.

We move down the plushly-carpeted hallway and step into the living room. It overlooks the backyard, which is a wide, green lawn dotted along the edges with brightly-colored flowers.

There's a luxurious white and gray-brick fireplace set along the wall. My inner heart claps its little hands. How long have I dreamed of a place like that, somewhere to sit with a cup of coffee or a glass of wine and read? In my last apartment, I had to read on the arm of the cramped love seat that was littered with Justin's corn chip crumbs.

No, I'm getting ahead of myself. This isn't my home. This isn't my place.

My gaze catches on the massive coat of arms above the fireplace.

Oooooooooh, fuck.

Ice runs through my veins, stilling my muscles.

It's a real life royal coat of arms. I read enough Latin to know exactly what all of this means. The hart, the shield, the fire.

In the periphery of my vision, Kasper and Mads flank me.

I can barely see them or anything else with the tunnel vision I'm experiencing.

"Lina—" Kasper says, his voice low, already reassuring.

"You're royalty?" I spin on Kasper, hands on my hips. Why I am so furious, I have no idea. It's easier than realizing I am way out of my depth. "Are you kidding me? How did no one at school know?"

Kasper shrugs, his hands in his pockets. At least he has a thread of good sense, as he looks almost contrite. "It's part of why I went to school in America. No one there knows anything about the royals outside of the U.K. And I'm not a king or anything. A lesser duke."

Hah. Was there weed in the smoked herring because I feel like I'm tripping. "Are you a Danish duke? This is too weird. It's like a twisted Hamlet."

Mads arches an eyebrow. "Hamlet was a prince. We can visit his Kronborg castle, if you like."

"No!" I swing my arms wildly in the air. I'm making a scene, and I hate it, but I'm flailing. Kasper is a duke? This is so much more than I am prepared to manage. Wealth is one thing, but royalty is an entirely different level. I've known several flight attendants who cater to sheikhs, and their stories are wild.

Mads puts a warm, soothing hand on my shoulder. "We're still the same people you know, Lina. The titles are old, they barely matter any more."

My eyes widen and I back away from both of them. "Of course. Of course. You're a duke, too. You're, like, duke friends. Is that your business? You sit around and vote on the best ways to crush the proletariat?"

Mads laughs, but stops at my murderous look. "This isn't the eighteenth century. The land our families used to own has been absorbed into other countries by this point. It's just a title."

I cross my arms over my chest. "Where was your duchy?"

Kasper rolls his eyes. "It sounds so pretentious. Do you have to know?"

"It's not like I won't find out." I'm not normally a terrible snoop, but I'm in the house of two secret dukes with some shady business, so, yeah. I'm going to make an exception.

"Kasper is from the Duchy of Zenstra, and I'm the Duke of Montplaisaince." Mads puts his hands into the pockets of his own trousers, and it's like I'm looking at male models on a magazine.

"Secret dukes." I fall/sit into one of the disarmingly cozy chairs by the fireplace. I pull the dark gray knit blanket around my shoulders. The jet lag has reared its ugly head. "I can't believe you are both secret dukes."

My eyes drift closed, lulled by the sounds of raindrops against the floor-to-ceiling windows.

"Get some rest, Lina," I hear one of them whisper. I can't tell through the overwhelming fog. But I do feel the soft press of lips against my forehead before I fall asleep.

CHAPTER 9

I don't know how long I sleep, but when I wake, I am wrapped in a thick, plush comforter that feels like crushed velvet against my face.

I yawn and stretch, my eyes gradually becoming accustomed to the dim light.

I'm in an unfamiliar room in a massive king-sized bed covered in the most luxurious linens I've ever felt. This ducal house is definitely an upgrade over my usual spare vacation rentals. Along one wall is a row of thick blackout curtains, and opposite that is a wall of chrome-edged mirrors. A candle burns soft light on the nightstand beside me, and the fire reflects along the row of mirrors as though there are infinite flames.

Now that I'm better rested, I can appreciate the perks of bunking with two dukes for the few days I'm here. I'm also completely famished.

I stretch my neck to both sides as I swing my legs out of bed. Something smells incredible, tangy and garlicky and rich.

Copenhagen might be my new favorite city.

My phone buzzes on the bedside table, and I check it, my stomach plummeting.

Justin, Justin, and Justin.

I roll my eyes and tuck my phone into the pocket of my slacks. Kasper and Mads are gentlemen, surprisingly. Though Kasper and I have already had sex, he hasn't seen me naked, and did not take the opportunity when I passed out in his living room.

There's a lot I'm learning about him. A lot I'm learning to like.

But that is a problematic line of thinking for a time when I'm not starving.

* * *

I FOLLOW the delicious smells downstairs, to the chrome and white kitchen. Whereas I've mostly seen this aesthetic as sterile, here it gives a cozy feel, like the warm sexiness of competence porn.

Not to mention gorgeous duke Mads standing before the stove, stirring a pot of something delicious. He's wearing a dark gray Oxford shirt with the sleeves rolled up, and a simple apron bearing the design of the Danish flag tied over his clothes.

A smile tugs at the corner of my mouth as I slide into one of the barstools at the hand-carved wooden island. "You cook, too?"

Mads spins, but he's clearly been expecting me. The smile he gives me is devastatingly sexy, sending rich warmth down my entire spine. "I took a six-week course in Lyon."

"The home of French cuisine?" I arch my eyebrows. "Fancy."

Mads chuckles slightly. "Of course you know about Lyon. Kasper was right about you. If you must know, I love to cook. There's something deeply satisfying about feeding people, watching them take their pleasure from my food."

He says that as he attends the meal he's preparing, but my dirty mind takes it as a double entendre.

"Well, I love to eat, so I'll take it."

His shoulders relax infinitesimally beneath his shirt. He's fit, too, with forearms like a pastry chef, strong and competent. "How did you sleep?"

I raise my arms above my head and stretch. "Very well. That bed is from another world. You should start a bed and breakfast if the whole club thing doesn't work out."

He turns off the stove and removes two white plates from a nearby glass-fronted cupboard. "Maybe. I'm glad you enjoy it."

I watch as he moves around the kitchen, clearly comfortable here. Before Justin and I moved in together, he tried to impress me one night by promising to make me dinner. He'd flitted around the tiny galley kitchen in his apartment, as though he'd never used any of the appliances before. Turns out he hadn't. At the time, I'd decided it was a charming gesture and we'd ordered Chinese.

Now, I realize he was a lying asshole the entire time.

As if on cue, my phone buzzes in my pocket. Mads, who has a bottle of red wine and a decanter in his hands, looks over at me.

"You're popular today. Before I carried you upstairs, your phone kept buzzing."

I sigh and place it on the counter. Two more messages from Justin. I delete them without reading.

I'd rather look at Mads, who pours the bottle of wine into the glass decanter, the liquid swirling and eddying and changing colors. It's like a delectable lava lamp.

"So, tell me how you and Kasper met. Did you used to jump naked in the Baltic together?" I mean it as a joke, but cannot keep the flush of heat from rising up my neck. They would look pretty amazing together.

"Not naked, but yes, we met when we were young. Both of our families chose the same seaside resort for a holiday. We became fast friends."

Mads hands me a tall glass of water, then goes to plate the meal. There's a rich, buttery-looking pasta, and a fresh green salad. Warm bread that perfumes the air. My dad learned to make sourdough when I was six years old, and the scent of homemade bread always makes me feel at home.

I chug the water. Jet lag is super dehydrating, and with the confusion and sex from earlier today, I'm more than a little thirsty. Mads refills my glass without question. No one takes care of me like this. Normally I'm the one bringing people drinks, feeding Justin, making sure my dads are okay.

This reversal is definitely appealing.

"Would you tell me more about your family?" I ask.

He sniffs the decanter and seems to find it ready, as he pours some into two wide-brimmed glasses. "What do you want to know?"

"The usual." I prop my chin in one hand and lean against the counter. Watching Mads cook is my new favorite obsession. He should have a sexy cooking show, Danish-flag-apron and all. I'd never get any work done. "Siblings, parents, et cetera."

He smiles and hands me a glass of wine. "There's not much to tell. I'm an only child. My father is a banker, my mother stays home. We see each other monthly."

A twinge of jealous guilt wrings my heart. "I wish I saw my dads that often." I need to see them. They're not getting younger. They need me.

"So your father is a duke, too?" I ask, to hide my own anxiety.

His lips curve. "Of course. But again, we really don't have

any authority. There is a queen of Denmark, of course. She is lovely. We are rarely invited to soirees and whatnot. Mostly, we just go about our lives."

It still sounds incredibly exciting to an American like me.

"What about you?" He adds some sprigs of herbs to our meal and carries the plates to the island. It smells like heaven died in a vat of butter.

I inhale the aroma of the food, letting it soak into my pores. There are tiny islands of dough in the rich sauce. A gorgeous Danish duke made homemade gnocchi. I can die happy now. "I'm an only child, too. I wish I lived closer to my dads. It's a minimum three-hour drive, and between my job and—other things, I haven't had the chance in a while." I pick up my fork and spear one of the gnocchi.

"Other things?" Mads swirls the wine in his glass, tilting it towards the counter nonchalantly, as though he does this all the time. I'm mesmerized by the way his lips curl around the rim of the glass, the soft stain of the wine against the pink flesh.

My core tingles, and my entire body heats. I am in so much trouble. Mads is appealing in a way I cannot contain.

My phone buzzes again and we both look at it. Shit.

"Justin?" Mads asks, one eyebrow raised.

"My ex." To distract myself, I take a bite of the meal and swoon. "Mads, this is unbelievable." It's unctuous and velvety and rich and lines every nerve in my body with warm, insidious lust.

"I like making gnocchi." He takes a bite of his own meal, then closes his eyes, moaning slightly. I swear I feel the hum along the sensitive skin of my inner thighs. "When I do something with my hands, it gives me a sense of accomplishment."

I nod and sip at the wine. It's a perfect accompaniment, just the right amount of acid and tannin to balance the rich sauce. "I get that."

Mads tilts his fork towards my phone. "What's the story with your ex?"

Of course, he's not going to let me get away with this. "Ugh. Justin and I went out for three years, lived together for two." It's best to say this straight out and get it over with. "We broke up yesterday, when I got a notification on my phone that he had posted a sex video online. With someone else." Mads whistles, a low, judgmental tone that I quite appreciate. "Exactly. When I came home to pack, he tried to make it sound like it was my fault. Asshole."

I don't want to think about him, about his stupid face and lame apologies. Not when I'm here, in this amazing house, with this incredible five-star meal, and this equally unbelievably sexy duke. This is not my real life and I want it. I need this fantasy.

"He sounds like a dick," Mads says. He takes out his own phone and types rapidly on the screen. "Now I have to see it."

"No," I groan, and reach half-heartedly for his phone. He holds it just out of my reach, teasing, playful. I probably shouldn't be getting hot from this, but my body doesn't get that memo. I squeeze my thighs together to hold in the lust pooling in my pussy, and let him keep his phone. So he'll watch a shitty sex tape.

Mads, though, props it between the two of us and hits play.

Even from the first few moments, it is clear that this is the lamest form of homemade porn. The girl sits on our bed, wearing a Moody Blues T-shirt, no doubt ironically. Her blonde hair hangs limply around her face and she pouts towards the camera. "Come on, big boy," she says. Hah. Justin, a big boy?

Mads eyes me. "Not true then?"

I bark a laugh, aloud this time. "Four inches, max, and he doesn't know how to use them." I can't quite believe I just admitted that to another man. I've never talked about any of my past lovers with a current one.

"I'm coming, babe," Justin says. He comes in from off-screen, his pale ass on full display. "You want me to make you wet, babe?"

"Ooh, yes," the girl says, biting her lip.

Mads props his chin on his hand and tilts his head, frowning. "This screenplay is clearly written by a master of dialogue."

I laugh again, and sip my wine. This is weirdly fun. I'd tried watching it before and all I felt was blind rage.

Justin settles himself between the girl's thighs. "I'll make it so good for the cameras, babe," he says, followed by a rather nauseating series of wet slurps and mumbles.

"Ugh, I shouldn't have had dinner first." Mads pushes away his empty plate, laughing. "He's quite terrible at that, isn't he? Maybe I should send him an anatomy book."

I snort into my wine glass. "You have no idea."

"She's not into it, either." Mads points at her face, where she's mugging for the camera. It's as though she is using it as a mirror to practice her O-face.

"Also unlikely to have a career with Hefner." Now the blonde girl is fluffing her hair with long pink fingernails. "Her O-face makes her look constipated."

Mads does a spit take with his water, then wipes it up with his napkin, laughing. "You hit that nail on the head."

"Is that good, babe?" Justin asks, standing from between her legs and cracking his back with a loud sound that reverberates in the camera's mic. "I'm going to nail you so hard."

"Oooh, yes," the girl replies.

Mads rolls his eyes. "I'm sorry for the years you spent with him."

I shrug, watching his expression, instead of paying attention to Justin attempting missionary and finding the wrong hole.

"I'm not sorry. Yes, the sex was boring, and he never asked me what I wanted." I turn briefly to the screen, where the girl is moaning but staring into the camera like she's trying to figure out what's stuck in her teeth. "We had some good times, though. It isn't all his fault, either. I mean, the cheating certainly is, but when I was with him, I didn't feel comfortable being myself. I didn't want to ask for what I wanted, because I was worried it would drive him away." I bite my lip. I've clearly way overshared.

Mads trails a single fingertip down my arm, leaving a trail of sparks everywhere he touches. "So, what do you want, Lina?"

My mind goes blank. I turn off the ridiculous sex tape. I can't handle hearing Justin say "oh baby oh baby oh" right now.

What do I want?

I look into Mads's soft hazel eyes. They're so inviting, so honest. Whereas Kasper is the pouty party boy, Mads is the teddy bear friend. Why can't they be one perfect man? Wild Kasper to stir up my kinky tendencies and Mads to come home to when I've had a bad day. It would be easy to love a man like that.

Which terrifies me. I don't know how to let myself be stripped bare to love like that. "I don't know."

"Yes, you do." The fingertip tracing my arm now runs the lines and curves of my hands.

I bite my lip. "I want what everyone does. Love and sex and companionship."

"And you don't think you deserve those things?"

If he keeps touching me like that, sensuous and sinewy, as though he's using his fingertip to memorize my skin, I might jump him right here.

"It's not that. I suppose I've felt a bit inferior since I went to Viceroy."

"Why?"

I drain my glass of wine, and Mads refills it for me from the decanter. "I never felt like I belonged there. I was a scholarship student, a local. I didn't board at the school, and the other kids bonded so quickly, over shared vacations to places my dads couldn't afford, or activities I'd never even heard of. The school was also so much harder than my previous one, so I had to study a lot, and I never went to a lot of parties." I swirl the wine in my glass, my gaze fixed on the legs dripping with impossible slowness down the sides. "I had a couple of friends, or one, really, but I decided pretty quickly that to survive, I needed to keep my head down and plow ahead." I bite my lip. "My dads wanted so badly for me to go to a good school. I never wanted to disappoint them. I still don't."

"I'm sure they're very proud of you."

He means it. Mads does not seem the type to speak in riddles.

"I hope so. I miss them." I sniff. Maybe after this next flight, I'll visit them for a little while. I deserve some down time.

I shake my head, wanting the easy, laughing, flirting thing we had been doing beforehand. "What about you? Where did you go to school?"

"Switzerland. Unlike Kasper, I quite like my parents, so I elected to stay in Europe."

Hmm. This was news. "Kasper doesn't like his parents?"

Mads shrugs. "They've never quite approved of his pastimes. It's a long story, better for him to tell it."

I stand and clear our plates. "This was amazing. Thank you so much. I'll do the dishes."

"You're the guest." He follows me to the sink, holding his utensils. "You cannot do the dishes if you're the guest. What sort of host do you take me to be?"

I put the dishes in the sink, distinctly aware of how close he is to me. He isn't crowding me, not exactly. It's more of a supremely pleasant proximity. Enough to feel in control and also aware of his powerful maleness. I turn, my hands on the countertop. He places his hands on either side of mine, his face inches from me.

"What do you want, Lina?" His voice is low, sensual, and it almost melts into the sounds of the raindrops against the kitchen windows.

Maybe it's the jet lag, or maybe it's the way Mads looks like every teenage fantasy I've ever entertained. "Honestly? Right now, I want you."

His eyes spark and he leans towards me, brushing a soft, sweet kiss against my lips. His touch is velvet and fleece, warm and inviting.

And altogether too short.

He nudges my nose with his. "Why don't you go take a bath? I'll finish up in here, and we can talk later."

Frustrated, I kiss him again, but he pulls back slightly. "We can't finish this now?" I ask.

He presses a conciliatory kiss to the pulse just behind my ear, and damn if I don't feel that touch all the way down to my clit. "Patience rewards with sweetness. Some things require time."

I sashay away, swinging my hips, certain he's watching me go.

Fine. If he wants me to take a bath, I'll take a bath.

CHAPTER 10

This isn't a bath. It's a private plunge pool, complete with indoor sauna beside it. I wouldn't be surprised if some of the jets spew rainbow-colored scented foam instead of plain water. I tighten the lapels of the plush cashmere robe I found in the walk-in closet around my shoulders.

Since Mads wouldn't have sex with me in the kitchen, I might as well avail myself of his hospitality.

I brought a glass of the red wine with me and I set it atop the bamboo bath tray. Beside that is a small jar of foaming lavender and chamomile bath bombs. Why not? Into the hot water they go.

I haven't had a bathtub since I lived with my dads in high school. It's never been the type of thing I thought I'd like. Showers were more practical, better for the me that is always on the move.

But my body aches from a combination of break-up stress, killer sex, and jet lag. So why not?

I hang the robe from the hook on the wall and sink into the deep white enamel tub, closing my eyes as I lie back. I submerge my body, letting the foaming bath bomb coat the surface of the water with perfumed lavender-colored bubbles.

My vagina, unused to so much activity, practically sighs in relaxation.

Whatever it is I'm doing here, I'm grateful for this time.

I hear the bathroom door creak open slightly. I left it ajar, on purpose, if I'm being honest. I bite the corner of my mouth, and hold the soft flesh there, curling it in my teeth.

"Lina?" Mads asks. I catch his reflection in the mirror above the sink. He's holding a lit candle in a smoky-white glass jar. "I thought you might like a candle for your bath?"

I glance down at my body. Everything below the neck is submerged beneath bubbles and water. I let my toes peek out. "That would be wonderful. Thank you."

He steps into the bathroom on silent feet, surrounded by a cloud of floral forest scent from the candle. I glance down and notice he's wearing a handsome pair of dark leather house slippers.

"No velvet slippers embroidered with your coat of arms, your Grace?" I ask.

"Haha." He sets the candle on the vanity in front of the mirror, so the glow from the flame reflects brighter. "Did you find everything you need?"

"You don't have to take care of me," I reply. I take a washcloth from the bath tray, dip it into the water and bubbles, and run it along my arm. His gaze snaps to my exposed flesh, and I smile inwardly. Jackpot. "Doesn't anyone take care of you?"

"I like taking care of people." He settles himself onto the bamboo stool that sits by the sauna.

His gaze on me is warmer than the water. "So do I." I sit up a little bit so the very top swells of my breasts are above the water and run the washcloth over my décolletage. "That doesn't mean it isn't nice having someone take care of me once in a while." I lean back in the tub, displacing bubbles, watching his hazel eyes darken. "What sorts of things do you like, Mads?"

He runs a palm over the five o'clock shadow on his strong, defined chin. "Good food, good wine. A hot sauna on a cold day." I play with the bubbles, uncovering my breasts briefly then hiding them again. He bites his lip.

I let one of my hands drift down my neck toward my chest, tracing the valley between my breasts and the line of my stomach. He watches my movements, though my skin is still covered by water. He knows what I'm doing, and it makes my clit throb. I lock my gaze with his as I settle my fingers on top of my aching, sensitive flesh, and rub. A soft moan escapes through my lips. "What are your feelings on a hot bath?"

The movement of my hand beneath the water stirs the surface in tiny eddies. I press harder on my clit and my back arches, sending my nipples above the water.

"Are you offering?" Mads asks, his voice coarse, like sandpaper.

"Do I need to write you a formal invitation? I'm a little busy at the moment." I rub harder. Having him watch me as I get myself off is unbearably erotic. The orgasm dangles just in front of me.

"I like watching you. You're stunning, Lina."

I bark a surprised laugh that makes the walls of my pussy clench. The warmth and wet against my clit feels so good. I pinch my nipple, and am rewarded with Mads's sharp intake of breath.

He stands and walks toward the tub. He toes off his slippers and loosens the collar of his shirt. "You don't think you're beautiful?"

My cheeks flush with the pleasure coursing through my

body. I don't feel like dealing with my deeply ingrained societal ideals of beauty. "I want to see your body."

He puts his hands on the buttons of his shirt but doesn't move them. "Why don't you think you're beautiful?"

Pleasure coils at the base of my lower spine and my lower abdomen throbs. I move my hand away from my pussy, pleasure no longer at the front of my mind. "I'm not. I'm fine, but I'm not like that girl Justin fucked on camera." The bitterness surprises me. I hadn't realized I'd internalized that slight in addition to his cheating, that he would cheat on someone so very unlike me. Someone rail thin and perky.

Mads stops in front of me, crouching next to me. With his thumb, he brushes away the tears I hadn't known were there. "She's nothing compared to you. I've never seen a sexier, smarter, more beautiful woman than you, Lina."

His words warm me, sending pleasurable curls to my nipples, my clit, the tips of my feet. The orgasm that had receded now ebbs back in soft, slow, slinky waves.

I bite my lip. "Can I see you now?"

He smiles and stands. "What other woman wants to see me naked before she makes herself come?"

"You're incredibly sexy, Mads. I like watching." Perhaps I should have said *you* but I mean it as I say it. Maybe I'm a little voyeuristic, a little exhibitionist.

A smile creases his face as the strip show starts and holy fuck, it's so much hotter than I expected. He unbuttons his shirt with infinite care, the heat in his gaze never leaving mine. Each inch of skin he reveals is better than the last, the hair dark across his chest and lining the muscles of his abdomen. He flicks open the button of his pants first, then drags down the zipper, letting the placket gape just enough to show his erection straining beneath.

He slides the pants over his hips, and that's it, that does it for me, I stroke my clit as hard as I can, and the orgasm is right there. I climax, crying out, straining my neck against the side of the enormous soaking tub. As I contract through the post-orgasmic waves, the water surrounding me shifts and pools as he slides into the tub across from me. I get a good, hard look at his firm cock, tense and veined above a pillow of dark curls. Not entirely meaning to, I lick my lips.

Mads chuckles and a flush runs up his neck. "You're amazing and unbelievable." He settles across from me, resting his arms on the sides of the enamel tub. It's large enough that our feet barely touch.

We aren't close enough.

I swim toward him, my muscles still soft and pliant from the orgasm. "Unbelievable good or unbelievable bad?"

I slide my arms around his neck and wrap my legs around his waist. If I lower myself two inches, I could rub his cock between my hot, wet lips. Not yet.

He cups my chin with one hand and uses the other to trace the length of my body, sliding down neck, shoulder, breast, ribs, and settling at the waist. "Good. Definitely good."

"Good. Can I kiss you now?"

"I've been waiting too long already."

I lean into him and press my mouth to his. His lips are velvet, pillowy and sweet like marshmallow frosting. I lick my tongue across his closed mouth, tasting the wine, the butter, the herbs from our dinner.

The hand on my waist clenches and he pulls me towards him. "Are you all right with all of this, Lina?"

"What do you mean?" I trail of line of kisses from his ear to his shoulder. His skin is salty and peppery, and it makes every part of me burn.

"With this." He gestures to the bathroom around us. "The luxury. The house. The meaningless titles." Now he takes his palm and presses it to the valley between my breasts. "With us."

"Yes. Yes, to all of it. May I touch you?" I grind my sex against his erection softly, accenting my question.

He moans, closing his eyes and arching his neck. "Definitely."

Thank goodness. I sink lower and wrap my pussy around his cock. I pump my lips along the sides, warming him, wetting him. He's so close to the entrance, my clit and inner walls are screaming for it, but not yet. One, he doesn't have a condom, and two, it isn't the right time. "You should know, though, unless the two of you have already talked. I had sex with Kasper."

"I know." His voice is more of a groan as his cock between my labia. "It doesn't bother me, if it doesn't bother you. He and I…like to share."

Relief gushes through me in a warm wave. "I want you, too, Mads. Please."

He yanks me towards him with firm hands on my hips and pulls me into a brutal kiss. Tongues tangle and plunge. Teeth gnash. It's a little feral and completely erotic.

He wraps my wet hair around his fist and tugs my head gently backward, bringing my nipples closer to his mouth. "These are perfect." He rims one with his thumb before he brushes closed teeth against it, sending sparks straight to my lady parts. I dig my fingers into his lean, strong shoulders as he devours my nipples, tugging and suckling and nipping, each sensation more than the last.

As he lavishes attention on my breasts, I rub my pussy along his cock, thrumming my clit with every slow drag. He moans against my flesh as his cock hardens even further. I wrap his granite with my wet silk, pulsing.

"I want you inside me." I lift his face from my chest and kiss him, filling it with need, with urgency.

He smiles against my lips. "One moment."

He stands from the tub, water raining off him. Fuck me, he is like a Nordic god, tall and taut- muscled and gorgeous.

He picks up his pants and pulls a condom from the back pocket. Within moments, he is sheathed and sinks back into the water.

"Where were we?" he asks.

In response, I slide into his lap and kiss those sweet lips, pressing my tongue into his mouth. I arch my back to position his cock at my entrance, right where I want him to be, and I slide down. Fuck, it feels good, the way his thick, hard cock spreads me open, the way I stretch and wrap around him.

I look at his face as I sink onto him until his balls rest directly against my ass. His eyes are half-closed, and he has this tiger's smile that makes me clench around his cock. "Fuck, Lina, your pussy is amazing."

I catch his gaze and hold it as I slide up and down, squeezing him with every stroke. His hazel eyes are dark and alive, and everywhere our bodies connect, my skin tingles. Hell, my entire body cries out *"Mads, Mads, Mads"* like a stadium anthem. I've always been self-conscious before, and never thought to watch my partner this intently. This has clearly been a mistake.

Watching Mads as his pleasure builds with mine is the sexiest fucking thing I've ever seen. I appreciate each twitch of his jaw, each stifled moan. I bounce faster on his cock, the orgasm so close I can taste it. *Mads, Mads, Mads,* my body cries.

He opens his mouth wide and squeezes my ass hard enough to bruise when he comes. As he convulses into me, he pulls me tighter against him, and the pain and pressure against my super-sensitized clit is enough to send me over the edge as well.

The orgasm rips through me, curling my toes, ricocheting

up the backs of my thighs, my spine. It curls me like a scimitar, arching me closer to Mads, and he is there, wrapping himself around my body.

We ride through the aftershocks that way, skin to skin, pulse to pulse.

I press a kiss to his cheek. "We've made a mess of your lovely bathroom."

Mads laughs, a full-throated sound full of joy and release. He doesn't even look at the minor flood outside the walls of the tub. His gaze never leaves mine. "Worth it."

$\mathcal{A}$fter he disposes of the condom, he joins me back in the tub. We refill it with hot water and add more bath bombs. We clean each other. He rubs a washcloth reverently over my body, and I massage shampoo and conditioner into his scalp with my fingertips.

Once we are clean and smiling, we climb into the massive bed together. We don't discuss it, it is a mutual decision. I am not ready to be done with him.

I cup his jaw in my hands as I lie in the bed facing him. "You are wonderful, Mads."

His smile edges into my chin. "I like you, Lina."

"Really?" I arch one eyebrow and pout my lips. "I don't know why, but I'm very grateful."

He tucks a curl of damp hair behind my ear. "Kasper said you have impostor syndrome."

"You should definitely believe what Kasper says about me."

He tilts his head, a furrow deepening between his brows. "You don't know? Kasper's always had a thing for you. Even back at Viceroy, you're all he would talk about. Every single phone call." He rolls his eyes slightly. "I suppose I can't complain. It helped me get to know you."

I sit up, the thick comforter pooling around my waist. "What? No, he didn't."

He laughs and tucks his hands behind his head, the very picture of satisfied male. "I was the one on the receiving end of the Lina Lectures. I would know."

"But he was *awful* to me. He called me everything besides a charity case."

"Lina." Mads sighs and yawns. "Kasper is many things, but he's not very emotionally mature. He can fuck until the cows come home, but when he feels a real emotional connection, he holds it at arm's length. It's probably why he opened Leather and Lace."

"Leather and Lace?" This is more intriguing than the confusing memories of Kasper in prep school. I snuggle into Mads's warmth. "What's that?"

"The name of our club." He meets my gaze, and there's something earnest yet guarded in his expression. "The original is here, in Christianshavn."

"What kind of club is it?" I have a feeling I know, but the idea of hearing him say the words makes my mouth water and my pussy tingle.

He holds my gaze with his. "It's a kink club. People can go there, to express themselves as they wish without judgment."

I want. My pulse quickens. Me, vanilla? Fuck you, Justin.

"Can I see it?"

Relief washes the lines from his handsome face. "Of course. If you like. Perhaps tomorrow."

Tomorrow.

A combination of jet lag, post-orgasmic fuzziness, and revelation fatigue weigh down my muscles. I nestle into Mads's firm chest, smelling of our bath. Tomorrow sounds lovely.

CHAPTER 12

I wake with a hard, thick cock pressing against my ass and firm, strong hands tracing the lines of my body. Well, this is nice.

My nipples tingle as Mads runs his thumbs over the peaks. I should always go to bed naked, if there is a man like this waiting for me.

I rub my ass against his cock, feeling the tip tap the skin between my cheeks.

Mads chuckles into the nape of my neck. "Good morning, gorgeous."

I turn towards him, covering my hand with my mouth. "My breath is terrible in the mornings."

"Hmm." He has a playful, pensive expression on his face. "I'll just have to kiss you somewhere else."

Before I can do anything but yelp, he has me on my back and he presses kisses down the center line of my stomach, pausing to lick into my belly button. I spread my legs for him and he settles himself in front of my pussy.

"I'm going to make you feel so good, Lina," he says.

Something sparks in my mind. Mads always takes care of

other people, but who takes care of him? I bite my bottom lip. "You know what would make me feel good?"

"What's that?" He nips lightly at my clit, sending shivers of pleasure and pain through my body.

This will not do. I sit up and pull my legs underneath me. I tilt my head to the side, letting my hair fall over one shoulder. Mads's eyes are dark and curious.

"I want to suck your cock," I say.

He shivers. "You don't have to—"

"You don't want me to?" I pout, tucking my shoulders back to make my breasts stand at attention. "I want to taste you." I get down on hands and knees on that enormous bed and crawl toward him, feeling like a goddess. "But if you don't want me to, I won't."

"I do." Mads sits up, but I push him back against the pillows.

"Good." I straddle his chest and bend down, pressing kisses down the line of his chest. I lick around his nipples, tweaking them between my fingers. The groan in his belly echoes through my body, the connection of his muscles to my pussy the conduit. I make my way slowly down his body, concentrating everywhere he clenches or hisses.

"Lina," he groans. I love the way he says my name, like I'm the rarest bottle of wine he's ever tried.

"Shh. It's my turn to take care of you." I slide down his body until my face is level with his cock. I lick my lips and a tingle of anticipation thrums through me.

I lick a drip of pre-come from the tip of his cock, letting his spicy sweet taste melt on my tongue. "Mmmm." I reach over him to pick up the glass of water on the bedside table and take a sip of the tepid water. I hold it in my mouth, warming it, then open my lips to take his cock deep down my throat. The warm water drips all around him, wrapping him in wet heat.

He bucks into my mouth. "Fuck, Lina, yes." He bucks again, the tip of his penis tapping the back of my throat. My eyes water, but he tastes so good.

I grip the now wet base of his cock and pump him into my mouth. I close my eyes, loving the throbbing of him inside my mouth. I straddle the hard rock of his thigh and rock my clit against his skin.

"What have I missed?" A low voice growls behind me.

Uh oh. I pop off Mads's cock and turn to see Kasper settling himself into a gray armchair. "Hello," I say. My heart is beating too quickly to say anything else.

"Good morning, Kasper." Mads stretches, the length of his thigh contracting under my pussy, and the delicious friction against my sensitive nub makes me wince.

Kasper nods. I search his expression for disgust or disappointment, but there's none. My pulse slows. He isn't upset that I'm currently sucking off his friend. He's turned on.

My cheeks flush with that knowledge, and I heat even more. They did say they liked to share… "We were a little busy." I pull my loose curls onto my head in a knot, knowing full well it brings my breasts into a better light. His face darkens as I hoped it would.

"Don't let me stop you," Kasper replies. He undoes the buttons on his shirt, one by one. "As long as you don't mind if I watch."

A thrill of pleasure surges within me. I turn to Mads and tilt my head, questioning.

"If you don't mind, Lina, I was quite enjoying myself."

Works for me. I release my hair, loving the way the silken tendrils fall against my bare shoulders. I bend over his pelvis again, but this time, I take each of his balls in my mouth, rolling them with my tongue. Mads groans and sinks his fingertips into my hair. "Fuck, Lina, that's good."

I flick my gaze towards Kasper, who has a wicked tilt to

his lips. Keeping my eyes on him, I lick Mads's thick cock from base to tip, coating him again with my saliva.

"You like that?" Kasper asks. "I'll bet he tastes good."

I lock eyes with Mads as I reply. "So, so good." I continue licking, focusing now on his sensitive tip, plunging into the slit with my tongue then puckering my lips and suckling the end. Mads writhes on the bed, trying to fuck my mouth with his dick. But I'm in control, and I can tell we all three like it.

"How deep can you take him?" Kasper asks.

Keeping my eyes locked on Mads and his deliriously pleasured expression, I open my mouth wide and take him deep. When the tip hits the back of my soft palate, I swallow. He flexes his cock into my throat with a grunt.

"That's good," Kasper says. I hear movement behind me, but Mads's cock is all I want to focus on. I suck and bob my head up and down, letting his moans guide me. "How is her mouth, Mads?"

He thrusts softly into my mouth again, his cock impossibly hardening more. "It's fucking amazing."

A drawer opens, but I cannot see anything beyond the pleasure building between my legs and Mads's orgasm. He deserves to be taken care of, and I deserve the friction from his thigh against my clit.

I suck harder, deeper, taking him farther into my mouth, wrapping my lips around him, making him wet. He groans again.

Then I hear a buzzing behind me. I turn slightly, Mads's cock still in my mouth, to see Kasper, his erection tenting his pants. He's holding a vibrator and a bottle of lube.

Excitement and anticipation tingle through me.

"Can I touch you, Lina?" Kasper asks, holding up the vibrator. I nod.

I bend back to my task, sucking on Mads like he is the

most delicious thing I have tasted. That's when I feel the first buzz against my nipples.

I cry out and arch my back, the pleasure intense and immediate.

The mattress sinks behind me and Kasper's scent surrounds me. "Don't stop. Mads deserves a little blow job, doesn't he?"

"It's not a little blow job," Mads says. His eyes are wild, his cock throbbing in my mouth. "Don't stop. I can feel the vibration in my balls when you touch her."

Oh, that does it for me, too. A gush of wetness rushes from my pussy, coating his thigh.

Kasper must see it. "Good girl, Lina. Now let Mads fuck your mouth while I take care of you."

So I do. As Kasper uses the vibrator on my nipples, the buzzing sensation itself nearly makes me come. He does that to me for a while, bringing me right to the edge and then holding back.

I'm panting, tears streaming from my eyes. I release Mads's cock, for the last time, I hope.

I turn, wild-eyed, to Kasper. "If you're not going to fuck me and you're not going to let me come, then go back to your chair and watch."

That wicked grin creases his face again, making him even more handsome. "Whatever you want, Lina. I like it when you ask."

He pulls a condom from the back pocket of his pants.

I turn to Mads while Kasper sheathes himself. "Do you want me to do anything differently?" I ask Mads.

"No. Lina, you are incredible. Keep doing what you're doing. I am so close."

Kasper picks up my hips so I'm sitting on my knees and spreads my legs wide.

I bend down and suck on Mads. Kasper runs a hand

through my slick, hot folds and moans. I arch back towards him, wanting to be filled, ready for it, needing it.

"So pretty," he says, caressing my ass. I feel his cock against my entrance and then he thrusts into me.

Yes. I close my eyes and bob up and down harder on Mads's cock, echoing Kasper's thrusts with my head. Oh, it feels so good. One cock in my mouth, another in my pussy. I am filled and it is glorious.

"Mads, have you tried Lina's pussy?" Kasper asks, his voice low and strained.

"Yes, yes, it's incredible." Mads is close. He's wild now, his hands deep in my hair, bucking his hips to thrust deeper into my mouth. "She's incredible. Look at her."

I suppose we all look. I do. I turn to the mirror and the sight I see breaks open something within me. There I am, the same old Lina, only this one has mussed hair, flushed cheeks, tears running from eyes bright with pleasure. One incredibly good-looking man in her mouth, another with his cock inside of her. I look like a goddess.

I watch in the mirror as Kasper takes the vibrator and sets it buzzing against my clit. I cry out onto Mads's cock, arching my back to take Kasper deeper.

"Yes, yes, more," Mads pants, and I oblige.

"You want him to come in your mouth?" Kasper asks, rocking hard into me, squeezing my ass.

I nod, desperately, the pleasure blinding me. Kasper pats my hip as he continues to fuck me. "Good girl."

I open my mouth again, taking Mads deep, swallowing twice, and with that, he comes undone, ropes of his sticky, sweet semen filling my mouth. I drink as quickly as I can, but I know some spills out the corners of my mouth. He fucks my mouth as he comes inside me, his cock pulsing and hot. "Lina, that's so good, so good."

I release his cock and lick the last few drips from the tip. Mads looks amazing, sexy and relaxed and sated.

"My turn," Kasper says.

He thrusts into me again, harder this time, keeping the vibrator in tight circles on my clit. Now that my entire focus is on this, I can't hold back the tidal wave of pleasure. With each stroke of his cock, each pulse of the toy, I climb higher and higher, sweet delirium closing in from the edges of my vision.

"You like that, Lina?" Kasper asks. His voice is hot and wet. One of his fingers dips into my arousal, and traces the juice down the line between my cheeks.

"Yes." I push back against him, wanting more, more sensation, more pleasure.

"What will it take to push you over the edge?" he asks.

His finger traces wet circles around the pucker between my cheeks. It's difficult to focus, with all the sensations.

"Put your finger in my ass," I say. I don't know where I get the idea, but the thought of it is tantalizing.

"Absolutely." He does, and the extra knuckle of sensation inside of me makes me buck and clench, and there it is, there is the wave breaking over me, flooding me with pleasure so intense it sparks. I ride it out, clenching around him, screaming *Kas* until I'm left boneless and shivering.

I'm a puddle of cotton, breathless and sexy and flushed. I collapse forward onto the mattress, Kasper's dick still inside of me, full and throbbing.

"Are you okay, Lina?"

"Mmmm, yes, so good."

"Can I keep going?"

"Yes. Yes, I want you to feel this way, too."

In my daze, I hear Kasper asking for help, and then Mads is there. He lifts me up and cradles me against his warm, solid chest. His soft, warm hands slide down my hips, and I wrap my arms around his neck.

"Did that feel good, Lina?" Mads whispers into my ear.

I cannot reply, just nuzzle into Mads's neck. With his hands, Mads bounces me up and down on Kasper's cock. I'm grateful for the help, as I'm too limp from the orgasm of my life to participate actively.

"That's it," Kasper says in a hiss, thrusting into me. "Almost, almost. Your pussy is incredible."

I look over Mads's shoulder into the mirrored wall. Is that me? Cradled between two impossibly wonderful men, looking full and sated and sexy? I think this is the Lina I was always meant to be.

I watch Kasper's face in the mirror as he comes, the strain in his neck muscles, the clenching of his eyes. How is it that I now find him wonderful?

When he pulls out, I am strangely empty. At least I have Mads in my arms, Mads laying me back on the bed, tucking the hair out of my face and settling me into the blankets on the bed. Someone hands me a glass of water, which I suck down gratefully. Sensation returns to my limbs in prickling instants.

These men are wonderful.

My eyes waft closed and Kasper's weight curls behind me, wrapping his arms around my waist, as I drift to sleep.

CHAPTER 13

I don't doze long. The blackout curtains hang just enough apart to let through a sliver of morning sun. It's warm and reassuring.

Plus, the smell of fresh coffee wafts up the stairs, and that's more than enough to get me moving.

I climb out of bed, naked. The sheets smells of Mads and Kasper, and while I could lounge in that cozy bed all day, I'd rather spend time with the actual men.

It confuses me, how I feel like I know them, and they know me, in ways I didn't think anyone would. It's like meeting them has unlocked a part of me that I had forgotten about, but I like her.

My muscles burn and ache in all the good ways. I wash up in the bathroom and pull my hair into a loose knot atop my head. When I inspect my image in the mirror, there are love bites along my neck. I leave them unconcealed. The sight of them gives me shivers of remembered pleasure. I find my slippers and wrap the thick robe around my naked body before padding downstairs.

Mads wears his Danish flag apron over a pair of boxer

shorts, letting all those lean, toned lines of arm muscle on display. Kasper is dressed already, in a white polo shirt and black pants.

"Good morning, gentlemen," I say, sliding onto the bar stool beside Kasper. He slides an arm around my waist, as Mads leans over the counter and kisses my forehead.

"You look gorgeous in the morning," he says.

"She's always gorgeous." Kasper squeezes my waist.

"Aw, you two will make me blush." I rub the back of my neck.

Mads hands me a mug of coffee, a small white porcelain milk jug, and a matching sugar bowl. "Hungry?"

"Starving." Apparently copious amounts of sex really increases the appetite. "Can I make something for you?"

Mads blushes. "No. I've got it. Thank you."

Kasper flips through something on his phone, frowning.

"Is everything okay, Kasper?" I ask.

He sets it face down beside his own coffee. "Business. I fucking hate business."

"No, you don't." Mads slices fruit with the ease and efficiency of a five star chef on a cooking show. It's pretty hot. "You don't like when things aren't easy."

Kasper rolls his eyes, reaches over, and steals a piece of apple from Mads's neat piles. "True."

I sip my coffee, which is so rich and full and delicious, I practically swoon. "Did something happen?"

"It's the club. It was popular initially, so we expanded to a few other European cities." Kasper places his two hands between his shoulder blades and stretches, popping his chest. My mouth waters. All this sex, and I still haven't seen him naked. Something like that needs fixing. "We expanded too early. So we are losing revenue. We need a new idea."

"What sort of idea?" Maybe Mads should do shirtless cooking demonstrations because it's definitely working for me. He slides a tray of freshly baked croissants from the oven, like it's something he's done a thousand times.

"Something new, something different. Something that will make a splash." Kasper stands up from beside me, and goes to the French press to refill his coffee.

"We've tried several things." Mads picks up one of the croissants with a pair of tongs. Working swiftly, he plates the flaky, buttery, steamy pastry and hands it to me along with a small plate of butter balls, and a crock of red, seeded jam. My hungry, jet-lagged stomach applauds. "We've held auctions, masquerades, other special events. They've all been successful, in the moment. But nothing has kept the momentum going. Nothing has driven the members to the other clubs, which are smaller than the flagship here. That was our hope with expanding, that people would travel and get their friends involved." He sighs, then slides the bowl of artistically cut fruit towards me.

I cannot reply because my mouth is bursting with fresh, hot pastry that's so good it's like buttery silk. The raspberry rhubarb jam is sweet and tart, cutting through the unctuous croissant.

Mads smiles, his gaze on my face. "I take it you like it."

"This is one of the best things I've ever eaten." At least I think that's what I say, as my mouth is still full of food, melting and sparkling on my tongue.

"Now you'll make me blush," Mads says softly, his gaze loaded and hot. Is he thinking about his cock in my mouth? Because I am, and that makes this my most favorite breakfast ever.

Kasper takes a plate of croissant from Mads and sits back down beside me at the island. "I don't want to talk about business. What shall we do today, Lina?"

I eat a slice of apple. "Don't you have to work? I can entertain myself." I don't mean it to sound dirty, but it comes out a bit like that, and Kasper tilts a wicked grin towards me.

"We would rather spend the day with you."

Mads brings his plate and mug, and sits down on the other side of me. "We are your local tour guides. What would you like to see?"

I ponder, warming my hands with my mug. "Honestly, I'd like to see your club."

The two of them exchange a glance with raised eyebrows. "Really?" Kasper asks.

"What? The other women you two have shared *don't* want to see your sex club?" I sip my coffee.

Mads finds great interest in ripping apart his croissant and buttering and jamming each piece.

"Not exactly," Kasper says. "We've tried, but…We met someone at the club a few months ago, and thought possibly…but it didn't exactly work out."

"How did it not work out?" A flush of jealousy washes over me. I'm suddenly desperate to know more about this woman, how she did not measure up for these men. What if they think I'm not enough either?

My heart, which had been wrapped in a cozy cocoon of coffee and blankets and soft candlelight, sinks.

Which is ridiculous. None of us have made any promises to the other. I'm only here for one more night, and then I need to go back to New York and figure out my real life. Kasper and Mads live this incredible Euro-chic existence, and I know full well I don't fit. I'm the townie, the scholarship kid.

I pull the lapel of my robe back over my shoulder where it had slipped down my bicep. No, this isn't my robe, it's the one I stole from the walk-in closet in this mansion of dreams. The thought makes me want to cry.

Kasper arches an eyebrow at me, but I play it cool. Keep it

easy. Light. He doesn't need to see the hurt underneath my exterior.

"She didn't quite fit," he says softly, his gaze burning holes through my robe.

"Oh." I smile, as brightly as I can, though his words warm me in a way I don't expect or realize I need. "So, plans for today? I like to see anything except portraits of self-aggrandizing white men."

Mads laughs. "We can handle that tour."

CHAPTER 14

We start at a food hall near the central train station, grazing our way through various smoked fishes, salads, and other local delicacies. Dill features prominently, and each dish is better than the last. Mads knows several of the proprietors, who accompany our snacks with aquavit or sparkling wine. It's more fun than I had anticipated. Mads and Kasper are so smart and witty and they match each other so well.

Mads has a personable kindness that thrills me. People gravitate to him, and I love watching his ease with the world. And Kasper. He keeps everyone at a distance, but he seems to want so much to be a part of something.

They're men it would be easy to love.

But I shove that down with draughts of liqueur.

By the end of the food tour, I'm pleasantly tipsy with a bursting stomach. It doesn't stop me from pulling both of them into a nearby empty alley and kissing them until none of us can see straight. Kasper holds me from behind, kneading my tits in his palms until I'm so wet, I want to beg for him. Mads cradles my face in his hands, his lips fluttering over my cheeks and forehead. I slide my hand down his pants, wrapping my fingers around his dick, and murmur into his ear, "Later. Promise me. Kasper, too."

He laughs huskily into my neck. "Anything for you, Lina." They release me with what seems like regret, and it makes me feel powerful.

We walk off our full stomachs on the way to Rosenborg Castle, which per Kasper was built as a pleasure palace for the famous Danish King Christian IV. As we walk through the dark walnut halls lined with tapestries, me giggling like I'm a third of my age, Mads regales us with saucy and possibly untrue tales of the monarch.

He points to a mirrored bedroom. Everything here is opulent, too grand, and yet completely expected after watching too many movies with my dads. "They say this is where the king kept his pornography."

I slap him playfully on the arm, and in return he cups my ass. "Don't kill the messenger," he says, nipping at my earlobe.

"Maybe I should just kiss him then." I press a light peck to his cheek. Kasper rolls his eyes. "Aren't the two of you dukes? Don't you have some behind the scenes type tour?"

Kasper shakes his head and leads me to a turret door and down a slightly creepy staircase to the room housing the treasury.

"What do you think?" Kasper asks, his breath hot on my neck. He sweeps aside my hair and licks the base of my neck.

I glance around, but no one is paying attention to the three of us. We're staring at a gilt necklace with a pendant on the end showing St. George slaying a dragon. "They're beautiful. They look heavy."

"Ego holds them up," Mads says. "That's the insignia of the Order of the Garter."

"Oh?" It's difficult to think of a witty comeback with

Kasper standing behind me, pressing his nascent erection against my ass, and Mads beside me, his scent overwhelming my senses. "To what order do the two of you belong?"

"Order of the horny." Kasper leans into my back and nips at the base of my ear. "How do you like sightseeing?"

My pussy is throbbing, what with the morning alcohol, the proximity of Crown Jewels, and, mostly, these two amazing men so close to me.

"There are other sights I'd prefer to see." I inhale deeply, warring with myself to keep my calm.

Mads's laugh is low and seductive. "We could walk to the Gefion Fountain."

"What's that?"

Kasper moves his hands to my hips and draws small circles against the fabric of my skirt.

"It's a fountain of the goddess Gefjon surrounded by four bulls."

"Oh, I like that image. Lucky woman."

Mads tilts a wicked smile at me, one that melts my already superheated libido. "The bulls represent her sons."

"You're ruining my fantasy."

Kasper laughs now and squeezes my hips. "We can't take you anywhere, can we, Lina?"

"Yes." I turn to him and wrap my arms around his neck. I lean into him and lick his ear. I'll keep my voice low. This is a public place, after all. "Take me somewhere you can fuck me."

I feel the crease of his grin against my cheek. "Is that what you want?"

"I want a cock in me." I bump my pelvis against him, the alcohol having sapped my internal editor.

Kasper sighs dramatically and steps away before taking my hand. "Mads, come on. What the lady wants, the lady shall have."

CHAPTER 15

Instead of finding a dark corner to fuck, as I had expected, Mads and Kasper have a taxi drive us over the bridge to Christianshavn. At least Mads has the decency to rest his hand on my thigh, his wrist rubbing against my clit, during the ride.

Now I am here, standing outside a newish stone building with a very small, discreet black and gold sign beside the door. I am also so wet I'm ready to jump either/both of them the moment I have access.

This Lina gets what she wants.

"Where are we?" I ask.

"You wanted to see the club," Kasper says. His face is oddly pinched, as though he is not sure what to do.

"Welcome to Leather and Lace." Mads nods in a reassuring gesture at Kasper, then takes my hand and opens the door.

The entryway is red velvet curtains, manned by a large enforcer-type man in a very nice, tailored suit. He nods to Mads and Kasper and holds out a hand for our coats, which we provide. The enforcer pulls aside the curtain.

My first thought is that I am underdressed. I chose a short A-line black skirt and a loose V-neck top this morning, which seemed appropriate for sightseeing. But for this place? I wish I had a siren-red dress, cut low in the front and the back, one that hugs my curves.

Because this place is beautiful, and from the moment I enter, I desperately want to fit in here.

The floors are a dark, polished wood that doesn't echo when the low heels of my boots strike against it. The walls are padded with black leatherette, and the tables and chairs are sleek chrome.

A bar of dark polished wood lines one wall, and opposite it stands a stage flanked on either side by heavy red velvet curtains. The music is soft instrumental, with a smoky, sexy undertone.

There are not many people around this time of day, but there are a few couples at the various tables. I bite my lip and lean into Mads's sturdy arm. The couple nearest me are two women, both impossibly beautiful, one whose face is bare of makeup but she wears an elaborate skin-tight dress that shows copious amounts of her glorious body. The other has lips so red they're almost black, and she wears a black Oxford shirt unbuttoned to her nipple line. The two of them are clearly into each other, their bodies as close together as they can be without actually touching.

"What do you think?" Kasper sticks his hands into his pockets and surveys his kingdom. He won't look at me.

"It's incredible." The two women near me are kissing now, their tongues tangled. The one in the dress slips a hand into the other's shirt, and her moan reverberates through me. If I thought I was horny before, it's nothing compared to now.

Mads hugs me from behind and leans his cheek against the top of my hair. "You're vibrating, Lina."

Not enough, not yet. "Show me around."

Kasper turns, his hopeful gaze quickly covered with his typical expression of ennui. "Come on."

They walk me past the stage. Mads explains how they hold special events for the members there. Auctions, presentations, lectures. "We had a shibari expert here last week."

I have no idea what that is but I have a feeling my internet search history might break later today.

Kasper leads us down a hallway lined with windows and low benches. "This is the voyeur hall. None of the rooms are currently occupied."

Mads grumbles, and I squeeze his hand. He glances down at me. "Like I've said, it can be difficult to drum up regular business."

"Maybe it's just early in the day." Though if either of them asked to fuck me in one of these rooms, I would one hundred percent be down for it. It does make sense that, as owners, they would not want to be seen using the rooms.

Which is both disappointing and highly responsible. Since I recently had sex at my workplace, I should be more understanding.

My raging libido does not get this logical message. It's easier to process, I suppose, than the eerie sensation that I might feel something very deep and very real for them. That's far more complex than sex.

I slide my hand up Mads's arm, touching the warm, firm length of his bicep. "This club is amazing."

"You like it?" His grin lights something within me, something that warms and soothes me.

"I love it."

He brushes my hair over my ears, cups my chin in his palms, and kisses me lightly. The warmth of his lips on mine feels so right. Like I've been waiting my entire life to find this sensation, and this is where I belong.

"You're here," a brusque, efficient, female voice says. I

turn from Mads and see a beautiful woman with dark brown skin and flashing light brown eyes in a perfectly-tailored black designer sheath dress. My gaze lands firmly on her four-inch stilettos, leopard print with a red sole. My spirit animal.

Kasper greets her with the customary kisses to her cheeks. "Yes. We are showing our friend, Lina, around the club. Lina, this is Asta Hansen."

Asia's gaze lights on me and her smile fills the hallway. "Lina. It is a pleasure to meet you." We exchange kisses, and I catch a whiff of her perfume. She smells like the perfect summer evening, floral and hazy.

"Did you look through the numbers?" she asks.

"Yes, last night." Kasper is all petulant prep school child again, telling the teacher, of *course* he did his homework. He sounds so jaded, whereas earlier today, when we were walking, he was all teasing and fun. "I know what they look like."

"Do you know what we are going to do about it?" Asta arches one perfectly-tweezed brow.

"Sorry, Lina. This will just be a moment." Mads squeezes my arm and joins their circle, the trio speaking in rapid-fire Danish.

I step away, unsure. This feels like high school. Wanting to fit in and knowing I don't.

I wait for a few moments, shifting my weight from foot to foot, inspecting the empty rooms in the voyeur hall. One is lined with mirrors and dominated by a massive bed. Another has an equally expansive bed with a steel grate overlying it. My brain and spine tingle with imagination.

At the end of the hallway is a room with a dark red carpet bisecting it. At the head of the carpet, in place of pride, sits a massive red and gold throne.

As I watch, the door to the room opens and the two women I saw earlier enter. The one in the dress backs the other up against the door, clutching her in a brutal, passionate kiss. Fire kindles deep in my belly. Should I be watching this? I suppose this is the voyeur hall. Still, I step backward a foot or two, hoping to shadow my features.

The two women don't notice. The one with the red lips cups the other woman's ass through her skintight dress, kneading. The woman puts her head back, opening her mouth. There is no sound here, but I can imagine it. A sensation that goes straight to your clit, a sound that rises from some primal core, begging for release.

The woman in the dress grabs the other by the lapels of her shirt and pulls her across the room, kissing her so deeply the other one has to hold on for dear life.

My clit throbs but my gaze is glued to the action in the room. I don't want to break the spell by touching myself.

The woman in the dress sits on the throne. She pulls her skirt up over her hips, exposing her sex. It makes sense, she couldn't wear panties under a dress like that. Even from this distance, I can see how wet she is. As if in response, my own pussy clenches.

The other woman stands before the throne, and slowly removes her clothes. First the shirt, sliding over the creamy arch of her shoulders. Underneath she has on a bra that is only a framework, her nipples on full display between patches of tape-like fabric. I bite my lip, my own nipples tensing and puckering. The woman runs her hands over her pale breasts, teasing her peaks until she tilts her head back and moans.

I forget I'm supposed to be standing back. I step closer to the glass.

The woman on the throne gives a command, and the other drops to her knees. Oh, yes. She spreads the woman's thighs wide, giving her ample space to work.

I'm panting. I want to see the moment, the instant when

tongue touches clit. I want to see the ecstasy, the pleasure, the wanton need. When it happens, the look on the woman's face is everything. I exhale loudly, my own voice a groan. I arch my back, feeling the slide of my sex against the fabric of my underwear. I shouldn't have worn any.

"You like to watch, Lina?" Kasper slides beside me, resting a hand on the swell of my ass. He follows my gaze.

"They're beautiful."

"You're beautiful." Mads appears on my other side and kisses my shoulder.

I close my eyes, reveling in their nearness. It feels so fleeting, and I want it so badly. "Take me somewhere." My voice sounds like it echoes from far away.

"Where do you want to go?"

"Anywhere with you."

CHAPTER 16

They lead me to a private room. It's not as adventurous as some of the rooms I saw in the voyeur hall, but the lighting is soft, the music is slow and sensual, and at least there's a bed and a mirror.

Once Kasper closes the door, I grab him and kiss him, then kiss Mads. "I want," I say, my breath heavy, one of them in either hand. I want so much more than I can say, than I will say.

Kasper laughs a little and holds me at a distance from them. "Yes, but we need ground rules."

"We've already done this. Avalanche, okay with ass play, let's go." I reach for him but he holds me at arm's length. Tears rise within me, unbidden. Frustrated lust and years of impostor syndrome. After the last couple of days, does this mean they don't want me?

Mads walks over to a cabinet and opens it. Inside are bottles of water, lube, condoms, protein bars, wipes, and a long black box. "How do you feel about toys, Lina?"

He opens the box and okay, fair, I had not realized there

were so many options. My eyes widen. I recognize anal beads, a rainbow-striped dildo, possibly nipple clamps, and a vibrator, but there are so many more. I touch a tapered glass toy with a flange at the base and a little pink heart at the tip. "What's this?"

The corner of Mads's mouth tilts upward. "It's a glass butt plug."

Oooooh. Lust coils around my lower spine. I realize I've spoken aloud when I hear Kasper's soft chuckle.

I point to two hoop-earring style rings attached to electrodes. I have a feeling I know what they do, but I'd rather the men tell me. "What about these?"

"Nipple stimulators."

"Hmm." I take the butt plug and the vibrator from the box and weigh them in my hands. "Aren't you two the nipple stimulators?"

Mads coughs and Kasper shifts his weight. This is *so* much fun. If I had known there were clubs like this in the cities I visited, I would have done this long ago.

Though, no, if I pause to think about it, I don't know that I would. Not without Mads and Kasper. They make me feel safe, secure, beautiful.

"If you want us to be." Kasper's hands twitch in his pockets.

"Good." I slip off my low-heeled walking boots and walk towards the mattress. Strange how I've lost all inhibition, and at the same time, not strange at all. With Kasper and Mads, I can be myself.

And this Lina is ready to play.

I set the toys on the mattress, flip my skirt over my hips to expose my ass, and place my hands on the soft surface. My pussy is so wet at this point I'm not sure we'll need lube. I toss my hair over my shoulder as I turn to them, what I hope is a coquettish smile playing across my face. "Which one of you is going to show me how to use these?"

They are with me in moments. Mads wraps his arms around my waist and kisses my neck. Kasper takes the hem of my shirt and pulls it over my head. Yes, yes, this feels good. Mads strokes his hands lower down my belly, then unzips my skirt. It puddles at my feet in a pool of silken fabric.

I'm putty in their hands. Kasper unhooks my bra and kneels before me on the bed. He laps at my breasts, rolling my nipples in his mouth then stroking them each, long and hard, with the muscle of his tongue. I shake and lean back against Mads's firm frame. He anchors me with one hand on my hip and the other sliding between my legs. His erection grows against me, and I grind against him, earning a groan and light slap against my aching clit. Sensation soars through me. I am wanton, I am needy, I am Lina. I arch into them, Mads's finger tracing wet hot circles on my sensitive clit, and Kasper's mouth on my tits.

"You are so hot," Mads says. He presses his palm against my clit to maintain the pressure and slides two fingers into me, stroking my bundle of nerves. I cry out, the pressure intense and perfect.

"Why am I the only one naked?" I manage. Kasper has a bottle of cold water now. I don't know when he got up to get it, as my entire blood flow has centered around my pussy and Mads's ministrations. Kasper takes a sip of water, then presses his cool mouth to my nipples. I buck and arch, the cool and hot temperatures making every nerve on my body sing. I thread my fingers into the short hair at Kasper's temples and pull him into my chest.

His laugh reverberates against my skin. "You first, Lina."

Mads removes his hand from my pussy and turns me so I'm sitting on the bed. He climbs onto the mattress behind me, his long, strong legs wrapping around my waist, and cups my breasts in his hands. "You like to watch, Lina?"

"Yes."

Kasper kneels between my thighs and slides my soaking wet panties down my legs. "You're so wet. What have you been thinking of?"

"You." Kasper leans in and blows warm, charged air against my pussy. I feel it everywhere. "The two of you." The word *love* rises inside of me but I swallow it and focus on the touch and heat and pleasure.

"Good girl." Kasper sets his mouth on me, licking, nipping, stroking. I can do nothing but roll with it, ride it, ride him. The orgasm builds quickly this time, starting at the base of my spine, sparkling through my core.

Then Mads has the vibrator buzzing against my skin. He touches it to my nipples and I buck and arch into the sensations. The extra stimulation stacks the waves of orgasm higher and faster, until it explodes from me. I grasp for any purchase, squeezing my legs around Kasper, reaching behind me to wrap my arms around Mads. The two of them hold me through my ecstasy, my much-needed orgasm rolling through every muscle and nerve in my body.

As the pleasure ebbs, and awareness sinks back into me, Mads carries me backward on the bed. He covers my body with his, and kisses me, plunging his tongue deep into my mouth. I cup his chin, pulling him closer. I tangle my tongue with his. He still tastes of sparkling wine and coffee and buttery pastry. I place my hands on the buttons of his shirt and work quickly. I want his body against mine. I want to be filled with this, with them, with these sensations.

Love. No, I tell myself. Lust.

"Should we try something else?" Kasper asks. I break from Mads, my lips bruised and bee-stung. Kasper stands beside us, his erection tenting his pants.

I lick my lips, and his gaze flicks to my mouth. "Anything," I moan, as Mads presses a line of kisses down my sternum, reactivating all of my pleasure centers. "But I want to see you. You and Mads, Kas."

Mads makes a discontented sound against my soft belly, but rises. His handsome cheeks are flushed, but his smile is relaxed and genuine. "Anything for you, Lina."

Mads strips first, making quick work of his clothes until he stands before me in boxer shorts. He flexes his pelvis, accentuating the hard line of his penis. He has beautiful legs, like a swimmer, strong and tapered.

We both turn to look at Kasper. His hands are reluctant, but when we both raise our eyes towards him, he laughs self-consciously and undoes the buttons on his shirt.

"Whoa." I knew he was toned underneath the fabric, but this is something else. His male V is well-defined, his abs etched like a sculptor chiseled them from stone. How often did he work out? His body is a work of art. "You need to drink more water, Kasper."

"Do I?" He seems emboldened now as he unzips his pants and slides them over his hips. "If you insist." He picks up the bottle of water he had earlier, takes a sip, then bends down and licks it into my still-quivering pussy. I cry and giggle as the combination of wet and heat explodes within me.

"Kasper!" My voice is light and teasing.

"You told me to do it."

He did it as a distraction, but I don't know why. He's glorious. I flip onto my side and gaze at him. "Why haven't you shown me your body before?"

He flushes and exchanges a glance with Mads, who shrugs. As if to say, it's your drama. Kasper sighs. "First of all, you rarely give me the opportunity to undress. Second…" He glances wildly around the room. "Some of the women I've been with have—well, I mean—" He shoves his hand through the hair at his temples. "All right. Many of the other women I've been with have taken one look at my body and made certain…conclusions."

I tilt my head, locking my gaze with his. "That you're only a body to them?"

His shoulders drop an inch. "Yes. A good fuck, that's all. Then they see the club and the objectification is worse. I thought, maybe, since you had known me before—"

I cup his strong, defined jaw between my hands and kiss him lightly. "Kas, I have to be honest. I thought I hated you for years. I thought you loathed me at Viceroy. But now I'm getting to know you, the real you, and I want to know so much more. You're funny and smart and self-conscious. You're surprisingly generous. The body is a nice bonus, but it's not a dealbreaker for me." Mads hugs me from behind, as though he understands how difficult it was for me to be honest. Kasper brings this out in me, the ability to verbalize what I actually want and need.

His strong jaw softens in my hands. "Really, Lina? I've always wanted you."

"You have me." I don't think about tomorrow. I don't think about my flight back. I can't. Not now. Not now when this feels real, and again the word *love* scratches at the back of my skull.

Instead of thinking, I press my body against his, my breasts flattening against the hard planes of his chest, and I kiss him. I kiss away the years of anger. I sweep my tongue between his lips and forgive. I release my resentment, and ask him to heal, to trust me. Maybe, maybe to love me. Even a little.

He wraps his arms around my ribs, pulling me towards him, skin-to-skin, chest to chest. He pulls his mouth from mine, changes the angle, and slants his open mouth against me. Plunging, taking, apologizing. His kiss is so powerful I bend backwards, but he has me in his arms.

Tears wet my cheeks, but they aren't mine.

"Kas?"

He buries his face in my neck, holding me close. "I've loved you for years, Lina. I was such a fucking shit to you, because I didn't know how to deal with it. I don't deserve you."

"Yes, you do." Tears roll down my shoulder from where he nestles, but I hold him fast. "You do, Kas." *Love.* I should say it back, but his hands are on me, stroking me, dulling all other reason.

Open-mouthed, he kisses along my collarbone, tasting his own salty tears. "I fucking love it when you say my name, Lina."

His touch burns in the best possible way. "I love it, too."

He presses me back on the bed, covering my body with his, the thick length of him rubbing against me. I shift, wrapping my labia around his cock, slicking it with the liquid of my arousal. His groan thrums through his entire body, rattling through me from my core to my toes.

He props himself on his arms, framing my face, and strokes his cock against me. Once, twice. Harder each time. I dig my fingertips into his sculpted ass, holding him closer to me. He isn't inside me, but this is intense and urgent. Each hot stroke against my clit sends spirals of liquid pleasure swirling through me, like the rush of rapids.

He kisses me, plunging his tongue deep into my mouth, deeper and deeper, his strokes faster and faster. I slide up the mattress with each powerful thrust.

The orgasm is there, hanging just at the edge of my vision. I grip his ass tighter, my breath panting, my entire body tense and needy and desperate, desperate for this, desperate for him. "Say my name," he commands, not breaking his rhythm as he thrusts against me.

"Kas!" I break, the heat and pleasure unlocking every reserved part of me. My muscles curl and expand, stars burst in front of my eyes like a thousand cliches and I don't fucking care because this feeling is incredible.

He kisses me through the aftershocks, but he is still hard. He hasn't come yet.

I kiss him, slide my finger around the perfect curve of his ass, and find his pucker. "Kas." It's a question, and he knows what I mean.

"Fuck yes, Lina," he says.

I remove my hand, suck on my index finger to wet it, then find that sexy ass of his, and slide my finger into him.

He cries out and breaks, his neck straining, the veins standing to attention. His back arches, his cock rises from between my legs, and he shoots hot, sticky ropes of semen onto my stomach.

He collapses beside me, panting, and plants a hand on my hip. "Are you okay?"

"Amazing." I stretch my neck and look over at him. "You're amazing. Just as you are."

A smile, a genuine one without teasing or sarcasm, tugs at his lips. He cups my chin in his palm. "Same."

Mads appears beside me and presses a kiss to my forehead. "Let me clean you up." He takes a warm wipe and cleans the cum from my belly. My sensitized skin arches into his hand. I'm still a little delirious, but the way these men touch me, it's like I can never get enough. *Love.* I think I might love them.

Mads finishes cleaning me, and hands both me and Kasper bottles of water. I watch Mads, his lean, strong swimmer's body flexing as he gazes at the water trickling out of the corners of my mouth.

I deliberately lick the droplets from the side of my lips, and I can see the way Mads's lower back twitches. My muscles and inner walls ache after the last few days, but I still want. "Is it your turn now?" I ask, arching my eyebrow.

Kasper lies on his back on the bed beside me, still breathing heavily. "I need another few minutes."

Mads only has eyes for me. I sit up on my knees before him and wrap my arms around his neck. His gaze is hot and insistent, like he's been watching us, planning all the things he wants to do. I nip at his chin, feeling his pelvis flex and his erect cock tap my belly. It's like it taps energy back into me. "You're not jealous, are you?" Suddenly, this is important. I thought we were all on the same page, but in this short span of time, they've both become so important to me. *Love.*

Mads sweeps the hair from my shoulders and twists it into a knot at the base of my skull. He holds it there, and tugs my head back slightly, exposing my neck. The kisses he presses to my sensitive skin send shockwaves down my spine. I've already come multiple times today, but it seems my body is ready for more.

"No. You and Kasper are both important to me. You needed to work something out." He takes my mouth in a passionate kiss, so different from Kasper's hard apologies, and so very, very sexy. "Do you want me jealous?"

His fingertips trails down my back, over my breasts. "No. I like you both." Though like is not enough.

"Good." His light touch is more stimulating than his hard kisses. Each flutter of fingertip against skin makes me shudder and burn.

He pulls away and inspects me, in this teasing, erotic way that has me writhing on the mattress. "What do you want, Lina?"

Them.

Hmm. The power is back in my hands. I bite my lip and think. My eyes catch on the vibrator and the glass butt plug I selected earlier. Warmth coils in my core.

Mads follows my gaze and a sexy, crooked smile creases his face. "Good girl, Lina." I watch as he walks over to the toys. He picks them both up and lubes them generously.

"How do we do this?" I lick my lips, excitement and adrenaline keeping me going.

Mads crosses the room to me again, cups my face in his steady palms, and kisses me, plunging his tongue deep. I war with him, wanting his hands on me, wanting his touch.

He presses me onto my back on the mattress, then locks my hands above my head. I frame his ribcage with my knees. Already I am wet and hot and panting for him.

"Kasper?" Mads gestures to my hands above my head. "Can you hold her?"

"Do you want that, duchess?" Kasper moves into position behind me, his muscles glistening with cooling sweat. He covers my wrists with his hands and a shiver of pleasure trembles through me.

"Yes. Yes." I arch into their touch. "Fill me up."

Kasper bends towards me and kisses me upside down,

licking my tongue with his, the hot muscle flush against my soft palate. It reminds me of the unyielding heft of his cock. It's new and erotic and I'm writhing now on the bed. More. I need more.

Mads kneels between my legs and lavishes attention on my breasts. My nipples heat intensely as he rolls them in his mouth and between his fingers. Fuck, I might come just from this.

Then Mads withdraws and slaps me lightly on the hip. "Flip over, Lina."

How had I forgotten this? Anticipation soars through me, giving my sex-sated muscles energy. I turn onto my hands and knees, and arch my back, sticking my ass closer to Mads's face. "Like this?" I ask.

"Look at yourself, you sexy duchess." Kasper turns my head to the mirror I had forgotten was there. I see myself, flushed and mussed and completely lusty, these two men whose gaze is on me.

A gush of juice rushes down my legs. Mads takes a finger and runs it over my soaking, flushed folds. "You are so wet. You want to get fucked again, Lina?"

"Yes. Yes."

Mads traces the line between my cheeks, pausing over the puckered skin. He dips the finger into my juices, then brings it back to my entrance. The wet firmness of his finger is tantalizing, and I arch into the touch, the moan falling from my lips.

Kasper catches it in a kiss. "You want that, Lina?"

"Yes. I want to be filled."

Mads dips a knuckle into me, teasing, testing. "Is that enough?"

"No." More. I want more.

I watch in the mirror as Mads picks up the lubricated glass butt plug. He positions it at my entrance. I bite my lip as

I press backward against the toy. The glass surface is cool and smooth and wet.

Mads settles one hand on my hip, while the other maintains a gentle pressure on the toy. "Are you ready?"

"Fuck, yes."

He slides the glass toy past the hard ring of muscle, and the pressure and pain are suddenly too intense. He pauses, letting me adjust and stretch, pain melting into pleasure. Kasper puts his arms around me, holding me upright. "You can always say 'avalanche,'" he whispers in my ear.

But now that I've adjusted, the pleasure at being filled overwhelms the discomfort. "More."

Mads slides it in another small amount, the toy smooth as it glides along the channel. "More?"

"More."

He works the toy in slowly, my back arching as it fills me. "Yes, yes, I like this," I say, stars sparking behind my eyes. I glance at the mirror, watching as Mads sets the flange directly against my opening so it stays in place. I purr as I wonder what it would feel like to replace the glass with one of their cocks.

"Mmmm." Kasper takes Mads's position and runs a hand appreciatively over my ass. "You like that, don't you, duchess?"

"Yes." I feel stretched and also empty. My core throbs with need.

"Will you stay there?" Kasper and Mads circle me, taking in the full picture. I stay on hands and knees, ass in the air, the little glass heart peeking out between my cheeks.

"Someone…someone needs to fuck me."

Kasper and Mads exchange a look, smiling at each other. "Well, you've already fucked me too well and I'm not quite ready to go again." Kasper takes a foil-wrapped condom from the assortment and hands it to Mads. "I want to watch Mads fuck you from behind. I want to see your face with that toy in your ass and his cock in your sweet, hot pussy."

My mouth drains of saliva and every part of my body overheats. I can't do anything but groan. Hopefully that conveys that I am one hundred percent on board with everything he said.

I watch in the mirror as Mads sheathes his cock and lines himself up behind me. He taps on the flange base, sending shivers of sensation through my core. "Are you ready, Lina?" I nod, and he thrusts into me, hard and fast. I cry out, the pleasure ricocheting and sparking through my body, sending me careening face first into the mattress. Mads thrusts again, rocking me into the bed. The pressure between his cock and the toy is almost too much, too much pleasure, too much sensation.

Mads wraps one of his strong arms around my waist, pulling me back onto my hands, and presses over my lower abdomen. That extra sensation makes me feel everything in one central spot, deep in my core. His cock, the tip of the toy, his hand. It's like one enormous G-spot, all concentrated on his touch. He rocks into me again, and again, and the pleasure spirals now, too fast to follow. I've never come this quickly before, but I've also never been this filled.

Wait. I lick my lips as Mads fucks me from behind, still maintaining the pressure on my abdomen, pushing down my womb from above, driving my cervix closer to the tip of his cock with each thrust.

I'm filled but not enough.

I find some measure of clarity through the fog of lust and arousal, and seek Kasper's face. "Cock," I manage through a dry mouth as Mads rocks the words from my throat. "I want your cock in my mouth."

Kasper grins and lines himself up in front of me. "As you wish, duchess."

I take his cock in my mouth, slicking it with my tongue as he likes, suckling on the end until I feel him tense.

"Lick his balls," Mads commands from behind me, not slowing his rhythm. I can do this, I can hold off the orgasm while I make sure we all get what we want.

I lick Kasper's balls, rolling them in my mouth. He threads his palms into the hair at my temples and groans. He's hard again. Watching Mads fuck me has gotten him so hard again.

Mads watches, and I can tell he likes it, because he speeds up the pace, thrusting harder into me. He taps the flange of the toy again, sending more sparks through me. "Swallow him," Mads says.

So I oblige, sliding Kasper's thick cock along my tongue until he juts at the base of my throat.

"Yes, yes, that is so good, Lina," Mads pants.

Yes, it is. I suck on Kasper and Mads fills me from behind, the toy stretching and tapping more nerve endings. This is what I want. The pleasure and pressure build inside of me, and I can't control it any longer. I don't want to. I break, convulsing, my inner walls clenching on Mads, drawing out his own orgasm. He thrusts into me as he comes into the condom. I try to maintain suction on Kasper, but I can't, my own climax saps me of reason and will.

As the aftershocks ripple through my body, I glance at us in the mirror. Mads's eyes are closed in ecstasy, his hands gripping my hips so firmly I hope I have bruises. Kasper kneels before me, stroking himself as he watches us in our throes.

I collapse then, the orgasm leaving me boneless and light and floaty.

Mads pulls out. He must dispose of the condom. I don't know because I can barely see anything. All I know is that he lies down beside me, wrapping his arms around me and pulling me close to him. I'm enveloped in his scent. *Love.*

Warm hands cup my backside through my post-orgasmic fog. Somehow, I manage to turn around and see Kasper, a wicked smile across his face. He taps the glass toy, and I squirm at the heady sensation. I'm so highly sensitized, any light touch makes me jump.

"Can I fuck you, duchess?" I hear him ask. I nod. He runs a hand down the valley of my ass, sparking sensation through me. "Can I fuck you here?"

Mads presses soft, healing kisses to my forehead.

Kasper slides the toy from my ass, and I groan at the loss of pressure. I hear the rip of a foil package, then cool lube slicks my puckered, stretched skin. Something smooth and hard taps at my entrance and, even in my fog, I understand.

"Yes," I say.

Kasper slides into me, inch by inch. He's bigger than the toy, but the way is slick and prepped, and I groan as he fills me with infinite care and slowness.

Mads supports me, holding my head to his chest, whispering something soft and lilting in Danish.

Kasper releases a satisfied groan as he sinks into me, his balls rubbing against my flesh. "You are amazing. So tight. So pretty."

I briefly consider asking for the vibrator on my clit, but I'm too boneless to open my mouth. Instead, I lean into Mads, loving the feel of being between these two men. Loving the way Kasper fucks me, loving the way Mads cares for me. I would give these men anything. *Love.* Fuck yes, I love them.

Kasper comes with a deep groan and collapses against my back, the throbs of his orgasm rocking through me, and through me into Mads.

Mads kisses me gently. "That was incredible."

Incredible feels like too small a word to describe what just happened here. Mind-blowing, life-altering, once-in-a-universe pleasure. None of them come close.

My eyes flutter closed, as I lose myself in the sensation of their skin against me, their soft voices blowing across my tender nerve endings. This is the one thing I have always wanted, and never knew how to ask for.

Acceptance. Love. Home.

CHAPTER 18

I'm dimly aware of the aftercare. The gentle cleansing, the healing kisses pressed to my skin. The bottle of water I drain, the protein bar I eat. Mostly I notice the feeling of coziness, of safety, the sinking into warm blankets, soft against my skin. The feeling of Mads and Kasper as they envelop me, wrapping me in their scent and strength.

I lose track of time, muscles and brain loose and lust-drained. We chat lightly between the three of us, laughing and soft. Mads purrs in Danish against my skin. Kasper strokes my back with featherlight touches.

Mads smiles and kisses my forehead. "Tomorrow we will take you to Malmo. We cross the Oresund Bridge and arrive in Sweden. We can walk the city, take you shopping. You can enjoy the architecture. The Turning Torso was the world's first spiraling skyscraper."

I smile into his chest. "Is it an enormous phallus?"

Kasper laughs. "Of course. You would like Malmo. A company there, Anonymouse, has built all of these miniature houses and amusement parks and shops for mice. It's very niche."

I picture little mouse shops, the tiny benches, the intricate designs. It sounds like magic, or serendipity, a tiny, lovely surprise if you happen to look in the right place at the right time. Isn't that how I got here, to this bed, to these men? Right place, right time.

I close my eyes and tears pool at the corners. Ice-cold reality gushes through my veins.

I cannot see any tiny mouse houses or phallic buildings tomorrow. I will not cross any bridge and spend the day with these men.

It isn't fair of me to lead them on. These past few days have only been a lovely fantasy. This cannot last. No matter what. Love? I am still just Lina. I don't belong here, sandwiched between two gorgeous dukes in a beautiful foreign country.

My heart breaks, but I swallow my tears and yearning.

Mads brushes his fingertips against my cheeks. "What's wrong, Lina?" Kasper stiffens behind me.

I cannot say this here, not naked in this bed with them. I stand and find my clothes on the floor where they landed.

I hear Kasper and Mads sit upright, the mattress creaking with their movement. "What's going on?" Kasper asks.

I pull my shirt over my head and yank on my skirt. I'll find my bra and panties later. As if on cue, my cell phone rings loudly in my purse. I fetch it, despair spiraling through me. Of course, it's a message from the airline, a reminder about my flight tomorrow.

Mads's warm hand wraps around my elbow. "Lina? Tell us. Whatever it is, we can help."

I switch off the phone screen, sniffing, still unable to look at him. "I cannot go to Malmo with you."

"If you don't want to go to Malmo, we can do something—"

"No." Why is this so hard? I barely know these two men, I remind myself. There's no way I can be in love with them, and they certainly are not in love with me. This was sex, pure and simple pleasure. "I can't go to Malmo tomorrow. I can't go anywhere with you. Don't the two of you work? Here?" I gesture around the room, suddenly remembering where we are.

"We are Danes. We work so we can live, not the other way around."

Why did that also have to sound so fucking fantastic? Everywhere that is not my life is so civilized.

Kasper shrugs himself back into his clothes, shielding that magnificent body.

Oh fuck, I'm never going to have sex like this again. I'm going to have to go back to the Justins of the world, faking orgasms with men who don't really know or respect me.

What did I expect? These two men are literal dukes. I was their weekend fling. This is not love.

I need to put on my big girl panties, and accept the truth.

It would probably be easier if I could find my actual panties.

I sniff and turn to face them. "I have to leave tomorrow. I have a flight from Stockholm to New York." I can do this, I can. "I have to go back home. I need to figure things out."

"You can't reschedule?" Mads pulls his pants back on. "We'd like to spend more time with you."

More time? A lifetime would not be enough, not with these two. The longer I spend with them, the more I want. It will be easier to cut the ties now, then get hurt later.

"I'm sorry." I swallow. "I can't."

Kasper takes my hand, and I stare at the conjunction of

our palms, the lacing of our fingers together. This isn't real. None of this is real. "Lina. Tell us what you want."

It will be easier, if I break this off now. I know, deep in my heart, this is the right thing, even if it is the one that hurts the most.

"I want to go back to the house, pack my things, and then I need to get on a train to Stockholm in the morning."

I can't bear to look at their faces, but I hear them as they move around the room, packing up, calling for a cleaning crew. Their silence speaks volumes.

CHAPTER 19

I sleep alone for the few hours before sunrise, though it's far from restful slumber. The luxurious bed mocks me with memories, as I can still smell Kasper and Mads on the sheets.

When I come downstairs, phone in hand to call a ride share, they are already awake. Mads hands me a cup of coffee and a shy smile.

"I can't. I have to get to the train station." It's better to be firm, so it reminds me to be firm as well.

Mads shoos at my phone. "Ridiculous. We will drive you. It will be faster. You won't miss your train. Unless we can convince you to stay."

A deep part of my heart twinges. I clasp my thighs together, grateful I am wearing trousers because my body bears the marks of these men. If I look at them too long, I will want to stay. I will want to abandon the old Lina, the responsible one, the one who knows her place. And I can't.

I am still her, the one who knows she isn't enough, the one who is a townie fighting for her place in a world that doesn't want her.

The fact that these men, even for only a few days, made me feel wanted and cherished…it's more than I could ever have hoped for.

I set the coffee on the end of the dining table and steel my spine. "Thank you both so much. I cannot tell you how much the past few days have meant to me." I go to Mads first, whose expression is confused and sweet. "Mads, you are such a wonderful man. You're kind and funny and sweet and I wish you all the best." I hug him, quick and tightly, but release before we take it too far. Kasper seems to understand what's going on. He stares at his coffee, the muscles of his jaw tense. "Kasper, thank you. Thank you for introducing me to this world. I owe you so much." I kiss the sharp ridge of his cheekbone, and he turns to me, his eyes blazing.

"Then why leave, Lina? We care about you. Stay. Let's try to figure it out."

"I can't." Tears well in my eyes. "I don't belong here, in this palace, not with you. You two deserve so much more. If I stay any longer, I'm going to get hurt. I'd rather the little pain now than the greater grief later."

Mads steps forward, but I can't keep doing this. "I have to go."

"Lina, please, at least give us your number so we can talk."

"I don't think that's a good idea." I pick up the handle of my suitcase and roll it down the hallway towards the front door. "Goodbye. You're both wonderful. Goodbye."

As I walk, I hear Mads behind me. He says, "*Farvel. Farvel, elskede.*"

I shut the door carefully behind me, then rest against it, sobs wracking through me without release. Deep in my heart, I know this is the right thing to do. I have to let them go, make a clean break. This world is a beautiful fantasy, and my reality is always bleaker.

CHAPTER 20

The rest of the day is a blur. The short ride to the train station, the high-speed rail to Stockholm. A pang twinges deep in my stomach as we pass Malmo. It will get easier. It has to get easier.

I change into my commercial airline flight attendant uniform at the train station before heading to the airport. As I undress, the marks on my body burn. There is Mads, there is Kasper, as though I am reliving their touch. It's almost too much to bear. Have I made an enormous mistake? I leave my hair in a low bun to cover the love bites on the back of my neck.

I greet my fellow flight crew, most of whom I've worked with before. The flight back to New York is surreal at best. My motions feel wooden, unsure, as though I am fitting myself into a mold that's warped.

My passengers mostly behave themselves, but there's always one. One who thinks he knows better. One who thinks I am there solely for his pleasure. When he pinches my ass, I whirl on him, fury rising in my neck. I see my fellow attendant walk down the aisle, so I keep my voice low.

"If you do that again, I'll—"

"You'll what?" The man grins like an overfed wolf, his double chin barely lifting. "You're not a princess, you're a servant. Get me another bourbon." He picks up his tablet, but makes sure to let his gaze linger on the swell of my breasts.

I want to slap him. The new Lina, the one who's just fucked two incredible dukes in ways she barely imagined possible, would. But I am also the old Lina, the one who needs to keep her job.

"I'll find someone else to assist you," I say, tightly. I meet the other attendant, Roger, in the aisle, and we don't need to speak. He knows how people act sometimes on flights, as though we are disposable, here only for their comfort, not for the safety of everyone on the plane.

Roger takes over that seat, and before I can comprehend everything that has happened, we are back in New York.

My phone buzzes as I walk through LaGuardia. It's Sarah.

Well???? Details stat!!!

My anger for her long ago ebbed.

It was great. No real details. Copenhagen is lovely.

As I near the exit doors to the street, it occurs to me that I don't know where to go. I don't have an apartment. I have other friends I can call, couches I can crash on while I work and search for a new apartment. All of that feels suddenly, completely, exhausting.

I sink onto a bench, holding my phone in my hands. It was the right move, to leave them, wasn't it?

Even if I may love them. It doesn't make sense.

My phone buzzes again, and it's still Sarah.

Seriously? Come over and we can talk.

I'm not ready to talk. I'm not ready to face this reality, where I am homeless because my ex-boyfriend is a cheating shithead, and the two men I—I care for are an ocean away.

I realize there is only one place to go. One place I need to go.

I stand, collect my luggage, and call a ride share to take me to Penn Station.

CHAPTER 21

ne Week Later

I sit on the wraparound porch, a glass of wine dripping with condensation in my hand. I've known this view my whole life. The chipped wooden railing that needs a fresh coat of gray paint, the apple and maple trees lining the back of the property. When I was eight, my dads built that swingset for me. When I was twelve, during a particularly nasty winter, we carved out a hollow in the thick layers of snow. My dads filled it with water from the hose and let it freeze, so we had a makeshift ice rink in our backyard.

Twelve-year-old Lina was no more an Olympic gold medalist figure skater than twenty-eight-year-old Lina. Maybe she was smarter, though.

I sip the rosé, losing the raspberry and peach flavors in my melancholy.

My phone buzzes beside me on the gingham seat of the porch glider.

Sarah: *What happened with KF??? He asked me at least four times for your number.*

I stare at the lock screen message. I haven't had nearly enough wine yet to deal with this.

It made so much sense to me at the time. A clean break after the most incredible weekend of my life. Now that the post-sex fog has lapsed into the ether, I can't shake the feeling that I made a huge mistake.

The screen door bangs open and my dad Kenneth steps onto the porch with the bottle of rose. "Hey, Lina love. Need a top off?"

I stare into my glass, which I've emptied at some point during my self loathing this humid evening. "Sure. Thanks, Dad."

He tilts the bottle in a generous pour then sits down beside me on the glider, holding his own glass in his hand.

"It's going to be a pretty night."

"Yeah." I tuck my feet up underneath me and rest against the sturdy wooden slats. "Only a thousand mosquitos instead of a million."

He laughs, the way he always does, with his entire body, the happy, full chortle of a man who lives his best life.

He quiets quickly, though, the joy ebbing so quickly it leaves me numb. "Are you going to tell me what happened in Copenhagen?"

I sniff. I know they're too smart to believe me. Maybe if I say it enough, it can still be true. "Nothing happened. I ate pastry, drank coffee, and went to a few museums." My body, the traitor, warms along my hips, as if I am back in the Rosenborg castle, their hands on me as we pretend to inspect the tapestries.

Kenneth arches one eyebrow but keeps his gaze on the backyard. Squirrels duck and dance between the boughs in the orchard. An evening bird trills. Music of my childhood.

His silence is deafening. "I told you, I needed to get out of New York for a few days. Recuperate after the shit with

Justin." It's the first time I've said that name in days, and now all it does is remind me of Mads, sitting beside me and making me laugh.

Kenneth sighs. "Lina love, I don't think you ever really cared about Justin. I can't help but feel like this long face of yours has to do with something else. We respect your privacy, as always, but you know how we feel about communication."

I laugh, a dry, brittle sound that doesn't belong in this hot, sticky, early summer's day. "Things that fester, rot."

"Exactly." He sips again at his wine. "So whatever's festering…"

He's right. Of course he is. I was blind not to acknowledge it earlier. I close my eyes, willing the words to come. "I—I met someone. In Copenhagen."

His cheeks flare with the hint of a smile but he coaxes it down. He and Rafael have gone to therapy for years, so they've long extolled the virtues of active listening.

"They made me feel—so wanted." I open my eyes and stare across the backyard where I grew up. A modest middle class life in the Berkshires, full of love and comfort. I never wanted for anything, until I got into Viceroy and realized just how far down the food chain I was. I always knew it wasn't fair to my dads, to feel that way. But I was a teenager. Much as I tried to deny it then, I was as much of a sucker for media propaganda and peer pressure as anyone else. I took my own insecurities and bottled them into a dislike for the Kasper Frederiksens of the world.

My dad puts his hand on my shoulder. "Then what happened?"

I gulp my wine. "I think I panicked. It didn't feel real, like I didn't belong there."

"Did they make you feel that way?"

"No." Even as I say it, I know it's true. "Never. It came from me. I think maybe I love them."

He wraps me in his signature dad hug, the one that warms me like a thousand hot cocoas and cozy blankets. It reminds me of the house in Copenhagen, and tears well behind my eyes.

"Lina love, you are more than enough. I hope they deserve you." He kisses my hair and hugs me tighter, letting my tears wet the shoulder of his polo shirt. "I know it was hard when you were in high school. We wanted the best for you, and it helped you be so strong. But you're not in high school any more. You're an amazing young woman, smart and beautiful. You can do and have whatever you want in this world. You just have to believe in it. Say it out loud. Own it."

My fingers tighten around my dad, digging into the soft fabric of his shirt. He's right. I can do this. If I want Mads and Kasper, I need to go to them. But I need to belong on my own terms, not only because they accept me. If it's more equitable, maybe it can be real love.

I pull away from him and he wipes away the tears under my eyes. "There's my Lina," he says, the pride so evident in his voice he might as well have hired a skywriter.

I nod, sniff, laugh. Hope bounces through me. "Dad, I have to go back to New York."

"Okay." He hugs me again. "Whatever you need, Lina love. But wait one day. Come to the winery with us tomorrow. Have some fun with your old dads before you manifest your destiny."

How could I refuse my fathers anything? "Absolutely."

CHAPTER 22

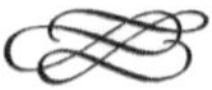

It's almost too hot for wine tasting, but my dads are having the best time, and I have no interest in spoiling their fun.

They're regulars and almost celebrities here at the local winery, so as much as they wanted to include me, I can slip away without much pretense.

I traipse around the outdoor sculpture gallery in my maxi sundress, a glass of the excellent rosé in one hand, a clutch holding my phone in the other. I need to collate my ideas before I talk to Kasper and Mads. I need a full, proper business plan.

I pause by an abstract sculpture made of tarnished brass. It's a miracle in itself, lasting outside in the Berkshires. Do they cover it when it rains or move it indoors during the winter? Or maybe the point is the tarnish, the imperfection growing each day, changing the sculpture, making it more lovely.

I glance over my shoulder. My dads swirl and swish their tastings at the outdoor bar, looking cozy and completely comfortable.

I'll have that, too. Once I earn it.

Footsteps crunch on the gravel path by me, and I turn, but it's as though the twisting of my body wrenches all the air from me. There, in the path, are Kasper and Mads, both looking so good I can almost taste them, can feel their skin pressed to mine.

Kasper's face is drawn, but Mads has a tentative smile on his face. He wears a light gray polo and seersucker pants with the cuffs slightly rolled. "Hello, Lina," he says.

I nearly drop my wine glass, but I maintain my hold on it. Desperate giddiness wars inside me with the desire to be professional, to stick to my plan. New Lina versus old Lina.

In the end, I win anyway. I set my wine glass on the ground, then race into Mads's waiting arms. He knots his hands on the small of my back, lifting me off the ground and spinning me in a circle like I'm the heroine of a romantic movie.

I don't care. He feels so good, this feels so good, so right. He sets me down and I turn to Kasper, my eyes sparkling. I kiss both of his cheeks in turn. He shies slightly at my touch, then sets a palm against my waist, clenching it. Like he can't believe I'm real.

"What are you doing here?" My heart won't stop fluttering. I want to hug them both, but a dim part of my brain registers that my dads are right over at the bar, and probably watching this entire thing. I want to tell them myself, when the timing is right.

Kasper's gaze slides over towards the groups of people by the bar and the outdoor games, all drinking and laughing. "Can we go somewhere quieter?"

I nod, then stand between them, letting their warm strength flank me. It feels like the last week I've only been half there, a shade of myself, and with them here, I can shine again.

We pick up my wine glass where I set it down, and I lead them down the path deeper into the sculpture garden. I remember there's a pretty bench set in a grove, not far from here.

There it is. A white iron-worked bench opposite an immense granite monolith. It's smooth and strong, its shape barely defined, as though the artist wanted the viewer to impart whatever meaning suited them.

I just want to see Mads and Kasper.

Once we all enter the grove, I place my wine glass on the bench and hug them both the way I want, the way I need, pressing my body to theirs. I close my eyes, inhaling their dual scents of comfort and reassurance. It's homey and sexy all at once.

"We missed you." Kasper rests his cheek on the top of my head. I love how I mold against the two of them, as though the three of us fit.

"I missed you, too."

Mads places his hand on the small of my back, the sensations flowing along my spine. "Why did you go? We tried to call you, but your friend—"

"Sarah." Kasper pulls away from us, his hands in the pockets of his gray linen pants. "She wouldn't give us your number."

My heart leapfrogs over my lungs and back again. "I'm so sorry. I made a mistake."

"Are you all right?" Mads rubs my back.

"Yes." I inhale for three counts then let my breath go. Time for my big girl panties. "Those three days were unbelievable. More than anything I've ever dreamed of. In such a short time, you both became so incredibly important to me. I didn't feel like I deserved it. I didn't feel like I deserved the luxury, or two dukes."

Kasper's brow furrows. "Did we make you feel like that? I thought we told you, that was high school."

"I know." I nod. This is hard, a little liquid courage wouldn't be misplaced. I pick up my glass and sip the wine. "The two of you treated me like royalty. And I—I fell in love with both of you. I realized, though, that I need to feel like I belong because I've earned it, not because I've merely been accepted." I exhale again, loudly. The realizations about yourself in your twenties are heady, delirious changes to your self image. "I've always wanted to be treated based on who I am, based on my merit. I don't want to walk into a club with you because you say so, but because I've earned my place."

Mads is nodding furiously, his dark locks bobbing. "Absolutely. That makes perfect sense. But Lina, we love you, too."

Kasper shrugs, but his frosty insecurity has been replaced by his adorable boyishness. "I suppose. I would say you've always proven yourselves to us."

"I want to prove it to me." Yes. I accept now that I got into Viceroy because I deserved it. I graduated from the Ivy League school of my choice because I worked my ass off. I chose to be a flight attendant because it is a job I love.

"So what's your plan?"

I sit on the bench and gesture for each of them to sit beside me. Kasper bends, nipping at my neck, but I shoo him away. "In a minute. I have an idea. One that will allow me to keep traveling, and one that will help you expand and connect Leather and Lace clubs in a novel way."

The excitement growing in their expressions is all the encouragement I need to continue.

CHAPTER 23

My heels click against the tarmac as I stroll towards the private hanger. There's a light breeze this morning, carrying with it the odd mélange of gasoline and daisies.

The hanger looks bright and friendly this morning. I hand my badge to the security agent, who smiles broadly at me. "Welcome to the inaugural flight, Ms. Altshul."

"Thank you." I clip my badge to the front of my red and black lace-print sheath dress and step inside the product of the last six months of planning.

A sense of relief and pride blooms in my chest, warming my arms and stomach.

Leather and Lace Airlines, the sign says in red and black curlicue font. At the desk, Dorie Jeffers and Asta Hansen applaud as I enter. I leave my suitcase on the lobby floor, then hug both women.

"Congratulations," I say, tears coursing down my face. I cannot extol the virtues of waterproof mascara enough. "You two are amazing." I step backwards and wipe the moisture from my face, laughing. "Twenty seconds in and I'm already sobbing."

"Don't worry." Asta strokes my back in a reassuring manner. "Everything will go smoothly. This is the soft opening, right?"

"We've all worked so hard." Once the three of us had joined forces to create Leather and Lace Airlines, it had taken all of our hearts and souls. It had also been one of the most enjoyable experiences of my life. I turn to Dorie Jeffers, now co-president of Leather and Lace Airlines. "Are you certain you and your wife don't want to take the first trip?"

"No." She smiles, in a secretive, soft way that tells me exactly how much she adores the woman she has married. "She has to work right now. We're going next. She promises."

"And then I get my turn." Asta's hazel eyes flare with naughty intention. "I firmly intend to take advantage of everything this airline has to offer. There's a huge benefit to being CFO of this company."

I grin broadly. My dads were so proud of me for starting this airline, they vowed to take one of the first trips, as well. I promised to save them a one-way from New York to Amsterdam.

"I can't tell you how many requests we have been getting," Asta says, picking up her tablet and scrolling through our reservation screen. "Every day our roster gets fuller and fuller. We need to expand soon to Asia. Maybe Bali, or Thailand."

"My wife has always wanted to go to Phuket," Dorie responds. She smoothes the lines of her silk shell top. "Any chance to see her in a bathing suit."

A flush of heat races through me. I've only packed one bathing suit, a lacy red string bikini that neither Mads nor Kasper has seen me in yet. I doubt I'll need it. The villa we're testing out has its own private beach. And I don't exactly mind exhibitionism.

The timer on Asta's tablet rings, and excitement courses through me. "It's time," she says. "Lina, the captain and co-pilot are already on board, headphones in. They'll keep the cockpit closed. Unless you want them involved." She arches an eyebrow at me, knowing quite well my own personal preferences.

But this trip is for us. For me and Mads and Kasper.

"Well, ladies, I'll see you on the flip side." I salute the two of them and make my way to the steps leading to our re-branded private jet.

It's gorgeous. Sleek and silver with our tasteful brand along one side. I step on board. Everything gleams with care and polish.

I stow my suitcase and rap lightly on the cockpit door.

Two chiseled pilots smile at me, their teeth white and shirts pressed. I nod at them professionally. "Ready?"

"Of course, Ms. Altshul." One of them winks at me, his blue eyes dark in the light from the cockpit. "Need anything?"

"Just privacy." I ensure they have snacks and drinks for the flight from Copenhagen to Aktion/Preveza. It isn't a long journey to the Grecian airport, and an even shorter charter boat ride to the Ionian island of Meganisi, where Leather and Lace, Inc. has purchased an exclusive luxury villa. One of many new destination vacation sites soon to be released.

Make Travel Sexy is our unofficial slogan. It's been unsurprisingly effective.

I walk the cabin of the luxurious private jet. There is ample champagne, top shelf liquor, and food in the galley. Plenty of lube and toys in the appropriate places. The seats all fold down and there are discretely placed rings for more adventurous play. Asta was particularly helpful with the BDSM arrangements.

I caress a pair of purple marabou-wrapped handcuffs and set them back into the toy cabinet. Last week, Mads tied and blindfolded me while Kasper engaged in wax play. My body still bears the delicious marks.

My core tingles. Six months into this relationship, and the mere thought of my men makes me wet.

It's not only the sex. Between the three of us, we even out one another's edges. They absorb my insecurities and make me see myself in a different, brighter light. Because of them, I can still do the job I love, while improving it and helping others see the world.

And have more orgasms. There's a reason this jet required some serious coating for its surfaces. With Leather and Lace airlines, everyone can enjoy the Mile High Club. It has the added fringe benefit of massively improving Kasper and Mads's business profits.

My phone buzzes in the pocket of my dress. I grin broadly as I read the group text.

* * *

MADS: *We're here. So proud of you, Lina. Ready for us?*
    Kasper: *Panties don't work under that uniform, duchess.*

* * *

I RUN my tongue over my teeth, the heat between my legs pooling and swirling.

* * *

LINA: *Let's keep it professional.*

Kasper: You can professionally bounce on my cock, duchess.

Mads: I can't wait to lift that tight little skirt over your hips. Love you, gorgeous.

He adds a peach and an eggplant emoji.

I shift slightly, feeling the glass butt plug inside of me move as well. A little surprise for the men I love. A little treat for me.

* * *

FOOTSTEPS RING on the stairwell and Mads and Kasper enter, each more delectable than the other in their fine tailored suits. It won't be too long before they're out of them. Behind them, the cabin door closes.

Alone at last.

I purse my ruby-red lips at them and extend them the cocktail tray I've prepared. Two bourbons in cut crystal glasses.

"Welcome, gentlemen." The corner of my mouth tilts as I take in the blatant lust in their eyes. Probably because I've already removed my dress, so I'm standing before them in my black stilettos and a red and black lacy teddy that doesn't conceal much. "Welcome to Leather and Lace Airlines, where we aim to take your travel experience miles higher."

Kasper runs a hand over the light stubble on his chin. "Fuck me, Lina."

I arch an eyebrow. "That's part of the plan, Mr. Frederiksen."

He reaches for me but I step out of the way, down the aisle. I gesture at the large captain's chairs. "Feel free to have a seat."

Mads undoes the buttons on his suit jacket and slides into a chair, taking the opportunity to run one of his hands up the back of my thigh. "We had a whole plan to spoil you, Lina."

"Then you show up like this." Kasper slips a hand around my waist and squeezes my ass. "I didn't realize it was possible to love you more."

"You can spoil me later. Once we reach cruising altitude."

I set their glasses of bourbon down on the trays, allowing extra arch so my breasts swell above the line of the lace teddy.

Kasper groans, and I note the growing bulge in his pants. "You're killing us."

The overhead speaker crackles to life, and a deep, rice voice echoes in the cabin. "Flight attendant, please prepare for take off. We have been cleared."

"Buckle up." I lean over and buckle Mads's seatbelt for him, giving his dick a little squeeze. "Safety first."

I go for the crew jumpseat, but Mads pulls me backward onto his lap. He must feel the little glass heart from the butt plug against his leg, because he groans and swells beneath me.

"You are a very good girl, aren't you, Lina?" He nips at my neck, sending shivers along my skin. "We are so fucking proud of you. Do you know how amazing you are? You built this incredible venture. You deserve all the praise today."

Warm pleasure runs like blood through my veins. These two always know how to build me up.

Kasper slides his hand over my thigh and squeezes. "Leather and Lace Airlines is going to be a huge success."

Yes. It will be. We've worked out all the details to ensure it.

For now, though, I just want my men on a secluded beach in the Ionian Islands.

Kasper fingers the tip of my clit through the thin layers of my clothes. "Can we fuck you now, Lina?"

The airplane taxis down the jetway, picking up speed. It's dangerous, me not being belted in place. But Mads's arm secures my waist, his erection grinding against the toy in my ass. And Kasper's hand is on me, too, his fingers slipping beneath the lace and into my wet heat.

As the inaugural flight of Leather and Lace Air leaves the ground, my orgasm, likely the first of many, peaks. I want them both, today and every day. I want my naked tits in Mads's mouth with his cock in my pussy and Kasper's in my ass. I want to cuddle with them afterward, me the middle spoon. I want to make them coffee naked then suck them off before we reach Greece.

I cry out my release as the plane enters the clouds above Denmark, cradled between my two dukes. Because they are mine, and I am Lina, their duchess.

* * *

WOULDN'T you love to travel with a bespoke kinky agency? Asta Hansen knows all about it. Read her story in Tied Up in Thailand. After being dumped at the altar, a shy billionaire hires Asta to give him sexless sex lessons, which of course goes exactly as planned once he learns she is a dominatrix.

* * *

IF YOU LOVED THIS BOOK, please let your friends know by leaving a review!

ABOUT THE AUTHOR

NC Ross is the spicy pen name for Natalie Cross. She writes about men and women exploring and enjoying their sexuality in far flung locales.

Ms. Cross lives in Los Angeles with a dog who resembles a chicken nugget (per her eight-year-old child) and loves watching cake decorating videos.

ALSO BY NC ROSS

Passion in Patagonia

Tied Up in Thailand

Auction in Australia

AFTERWORD

I hope you love reading as much as I do. If you have any feedback or just want to chat travel destinations, check out my website and let me know.

www.ingramcontent.com/pod-product-compliance
Lightning Source LLC
Chambersburg PA
CBHW031410310726
48971CB00003B/814